'INSPIRING SOULS'

Gille Sidhu

INTRODUCTION

True life stories can be tragic, sad, happy, the list goes on. Everyone has a different story to tell, some stories may have the same connotation as the next person but a different outcome. Not everyone copes with what life throws at them. This book is about the challenging times some people go through or some challenging roles they have taken on helping them to come out as stronger people. What gives them the strength to carry on in life after such tragic circumstances, what inspires them to change their jobs, give up drugs, live with a with a life-threatening condition, deal with chronic pain, and escape from abusive relationships etc. Maybe there is an unknown factor in the air which determines our outcome. Can we learn from the stories that others share with us, delve deep into their soul and how they became the stronger people they are?

Many people will say I was inspired because…? What exactly inspired you? Did someone inspire you? Were you so inspired that you made a change in your life? Maybe you are the inspiration to others. Maybe we all possess an inner strength.

How many people do each of us inspire, and how many people have inspired us? It may be the teacher who could motivate a class and get the best results from each of her pupils; how did the teacher do it? It could be a parent or a friend, a stranger we met, an idol, or it could simply be that inspiring story that stood the test of time.

Beautiful individual stories with different styles of writing, straight from the soul, on true-life inspiring stories by people in all walks of life. Every story is unique.

The stories are written by many writers, some writers for personal reasons wish their names to remain anonymous in this book. One author wanted to remain anonymous because he liked being mysterious.

Table of Contents

A Strong Heart

Tas

When I was young, I always knew there was something unique about my Uncle Sebastian, the way my family adored him and his friends admired him. I could tell he was special. When I grew older, my Grandmother told me the story of his extraordinary courage in life and why we were all so lucky to have him here.

It began on the 8th of February 1970 when Sebastian came into this world. Being the youngest of her five children, my Grandmother, Margaret, knew instantly that something was wrong when she couldn't hear her baby cry exhausted and panicked, she could do nothing as the nurses rushed him away, a tiny blue foot hanging from the white towel he was wrapped in. When the midwife returned, she said, "don't learn to love him, dear" as she handed the baby over "he won't be here for long".

Margaret stared at her baby as he struggled for every sharp, short breath. Her heart filled with joy and terror all at once. She clung to her child for three hours before a doctor came to see her. His face was emotionless as he explained the child had been born with congenital heart disease. He called it "a weak heart, a heart that could not support his tiny body for longer than a day."

Three days later, much to everyone's surprise, Sebastian and his mother were sent home. The doctor continued to reiterate the seriousness of his condition and assured Margaret that it would be a miracle if her baby should live for six months. One year later, Sebastian began to walk. In these initial years, this little boy made it clear to everyone he was going to fight for his life. Time after time, he baffled medical professionals who claimed that every day he woke up was a medical phenomenon. It was beginning to seem like he had defied the odds until eventually, his heart was almost ready to give in. My Grandparents were faced with an impossible decision, but Sebastian had only one option.

It is known as the Mustard procedure, and today it has saved many young lives however, in 1973, this was not the case.

Sebastian would be the youngest patient in Australia to ever undergo this surgery and doctors at the time were less than optimistic about his survival. My grandparents had to take a leap of faith this was decision that could change their lives forever but it was their only chance.

Sebastian survived his first major open-heart surgery at the age of three. His doctors were in uncharted waters and being so young they were unsure of what his recovery would look like or if he would recover at all. My Grandparents were told he could never have a normal childhood, he mustn't run, he mustn't play and he definitely mustn't ever attend a regular school. Still, with 5 kids, a big backyard and long Australian summers, there was plenty of fun to be had and Sebastian was sure not to miss out on a single bit of it. My Grandmother dealt with grazed knees, muddy hands and torn shorts just like she had with her four children before him. At the age of six, Sebastian was preparing for his first day at the local primary school.

It was orientation day when my Grandmother was pulled aside by the headteacher. Although his intentions were good, his efforts were misplaced when he tried to sway her from enrolling Sebastian. He was concerned there may be bullying and assumed that Sebastian was a delicate, easily spooked child. By now my Grandmother was used to people underestimating her son but she was also used to him proving them wrong almost every time and was secretly delighted when she watched him turn those bullies into friends on day one.

A few years passed, and Sebastian was still doing well. Again, the doctors tried to estimate his life expectancy and twenty years was the new number. A little older now, he began to understand what this all meant. Not wanting to take any chances he began living every year he had to it's absolute fullest. Throughout his teenage years Sebastian was on the soccer team, the cricket team and the swim team, he learnt to surf, to skateboard and eventually how to ride a motorcycle. Once his twentieth birthday came and went, he travelled the world and lived all over the country before he eventually settled in a small town on the east coast. A town my Mum and Sebastian had spent many summers visiting their older brothers when they were just teenagers. A sleepy place called

Byron bay with incredible beaches set against a backdrop of rainforest-covered mountains.

At the time it was no more than a holiday destination, but after having me, my Mum decided she was going back to university and left the busy suburbs of Sydney to move to a quiet house in a quiet place, Byron Bay seemed like the perfect fit. 6 months later Sebastian joined us, here he became a jewelry maker and worked in a lighthouse at the most easterly point of Australia. He spent his days enjoying incredible ocean views, fiery sunsets and whale watching with visitors from across the globe.

For years I didn't know any of this about my uncle but while I was growing up, he was always the calm amongst the storm, he saw life with humour and enjoyed every day rain or shine. He had time for me when the other adults were too busy, he pushed me hardest when I was scared, he taught me how to laugh even when things felt bad and he made sure I don't let anyone else tell me what I am capable of.

Sebastian has now been waiting on the heart transplant list for three years and we're hoping he will receive a heart soon but he will also be turning fifty this year which for someone who was giving only 24 hours to live half a century ago feels like a pretty huge bonus and I know he has cherished every second of it.

A Changing Life

Anonymous

Life can take its twists and turns as we know. Sometimes something can come along so unexpectedly to change the course of our lives in a way that had never been imagined.

My life hadn't been easy perhaps much like most lives but I had learnt to become independent, confident in my work, satisfied with my life as it was. I have always been a particularly shy, nervous person but through my work I learnt to be stronger. I worked in a healthcare setting; a prestigious job where I was depended upon and could cope with whatever the job required.

So, it came as a bit of a shock when suddenly I started to feel unsure of myself, coming home feeling I wasn't coping, only wanting to eat and go straight to bed. It wasn't like me but I wasn't concerned. I just thought I was tired. Until suddenly it came to me that I needed time away from work. It was a strong feeling that just wouldn't go away. I approached my manager and organised a six-week sabbatical.

Initially I felt a freedom that was euphoric. But soon I found the days hard to get through and was unable to concentrate on anything. It came to me just as suddenly as before that I needed to see a doctor and I didn't know why. On the day of the appointment I knew my husband had to come with me. I probably cried for a week continuously after that appointment. A few days later after my initial appointment I found it difficult to get out of bed and that evening I couldn't feed myself. My husband had to bathe me and put me to bed. The next day he had to dress me and take me to the doctor. At this point I couldn't put one foot in front of the other. He had to move my legs for me to get me to walk into the surgery. The receptionist took one look at me and took me straight through. The doctor was concerned by what had happened to me and told my husband he was calling an ambulance. My recollections of that day are vague but I remember being fixated on a spot on the ceiling and then an ambulance man putting his face so close to mine that I felt uncomfortable. I could sense he was trying to reassure me but instead he was scaring me. I couldn't put my trust in him. I was afraid to go with him but I was unable to make any decisions. I was carried into the ambulance where I was questioned as to whether I'd taken any drugs which I hadn't. I recall telling the paramedic there was no way I would've taken an overdose as my brother had done that many years ago and I tried to save him but failed. Yet I felt they were accusing me of doing this to myself.

I was wheeled along the corridor feeling frightened I was going to a psychiatric unit. Having been a nurse I knew what those places were like. The nurse undressed me and my body seemed odorous and disgusting.

The day is blurry in my memory although I remember hearing the doctor say "she's had a nervous breakdown". I wasn't sure who she was talking about. My husband had gone home and I felt very alone in a strange place where I was unsure what was going to happen. I didn't know what was wrong with me but I didn't have a need to know.

The next day I vomited quite violently although I hadn't been eating. My body felt tired leaving me feeling different. My brain was unable to process information or make sense of anything. My husband said I had to see a psychiatrist before they would consider letting me home. I felt a desperate urge to get out of the hospital and back to familiar surroundings. The psychiatrist asked lots of questions making me feel like someone wanted to listen to me and help me. At the end of the consultation my disappointment returned as realisation hit me that he wasn't going to help and that he was just going through a routine familiar to him.

My husband took me away for a break somewhere but I felt out of my depth. I needed familiarity. Yet on our return home I became anxious and very tearful as I remembered the feelings I had when I left the hospital and was afraid, I couldn't escape those feelings.

The days after that became monotonous. I did nothing but wash and dress myself. I barely ate. I had no energy, no motivation, no understanding of other's feelings and no wish to talk to anyone. My pulse would race if the phone rang. Going out in the car, the noise of the traffic was unbearable. I couldn't listen to music, it sounded distorted and loud whatever the volume. I had overwhelming feelings of needing to cocoon myself, be alone, cut off from the outside world. Yet I watched the clock until my husband returned from work. I was totally dependent on him. I remember that summer as being cold when, in actual fact, it was a very hot summer but I barely ventured outside. I couldn't shake off the feeling that I shouldn't be in this world. I became afraid of open windows upstairs and visualised myself falling out. The stairs were difficult as I could always see myself lying at the bottom dead! I had no suicide plan at that time just this overwhelming feeling that it was going to happen.

But the worst thing was the thoughts in my head. I had what I can only describe as, a video recorder inside my head that kept playing and stopping at different points, then rewinding and playing again. Events of my life I didn't want to remember were in vivid detail. I had no control over these thoughts, it was difficult to distract myself away from them. Thoughts that were very disturbing and real.

I began seeing a psychologist who really did listen to me. She let me talk about anything. I clung to those appointments......

My husband and friends took me out, they were very understanding. I felt a burden to them, and would try to be cheerful when with them, but couldn't wait to get back to my sanctuary at home. Gradually their perseverance started paying off and I felt more at ease about going out.

I'd always liked walking and I began to see the benefits of this again as my energy levels returned. The beauty of nature began to sit well with me giving me a feeling of calmness.

Work was not on my mind for many months. The GP gave me as much sick time as I required. It was about 7 months later when I thought that I would need to consider whether I was going back to work or not since my husband and I had made a provisional plan for our retirement which involved me working for a few more years.

Gradually I started to see that I didn't want to give up on all my years of training and just 'throw in the towel'. I was starting to get better. I was more able to go into a shop without running out. I'd always loved shopping but I couldn't bear the noise of people around me. So, could I now be able to face work where I had to see and talk to many people in the course of a day? I also needed to feel I could be 'on the ball' and able to use my skills. I discussed my return with my manager via emails (I didn't feel able to see her at that time). She was incredibly supportive, as she had always been, and helped to find a way for me to gradually return to my duties initially doing office work to avoid the 'face to face'....

I cried immediately as I went through the doors at work but luckily a colleague met me and helped me. I worked in an office for quite a while and started to enjoy the company of the others that were there. Everyone was very kind and considerate. I felt ashamed that I had needed that.

I had an incredibly painful menstrual period during my office time. It reminded me that I hadn't had that for a while. Yet I often had dysmenorrhea (painful periods) to the extent where I needed very strong painkillers to relieve the pain. I had my 50th birthday around this time.

I started to do some research as I began to wonder about my hormone levels. I had always had premenstrual syndrome, postnatal depression and the aforementioned dysmenorrhea. But my periods were regular; I was certain I was not entering the menopause. I had no symptoms, no hot flushes or other signs. At least I didn't think I did...

I checked my hormone levels but they weren't obviously indicative of menopause yet it's notoriously difficult to diagnose it that way. I worked with gynaecologists, one or two knew some of my situation - no one suggested having my hormones checked.

Returning to my job reinforced my presence in the world and my usefulness which helped give me the identity that had been missing for such a long time. I'm very grateful I was able to return to work in the way that I did otherwise I may have just left and never got out of a cycle of low self-esteem and self-worth.

It took many years to get back on a path that was conducive to a 'normal' existence but I have never got back to where I was. The demons stayed for a long time. Obviously with age we accept some things will change. I tried many treatments whether conventional or more homeopathic but my salvation came from a chance conversation and a call to a private doctor

A very very old (way past retirement) doctor who was very very old fashioned had written research papers about women like myself who suffered from sensitivity to hormone changes. These women could suffer from a premenopausal phase. The clue had been my history of premenstrual syndrome and post-natal depression. He prescribed a formula that changed my life but it came nine years after my problems started. My local doctor had tried different antidepressants and different hormonal medication but some made me go back towards the situation I had been in. This told me the problem was definitely hormonal. It was surprising to me that no one around me (even though I was working in a hospital) had mentioned it. My sister, with no medical knowledge, said to me 'I bet it's the menopause' as she went through something similar after me. I later discovered it runs strongly in my family and that there were great aunts who had been detained in asylums for years, suffering undignified treatments, with a diagnosis of 'madness'. Modern medicine saved me and helped me towards the road of recovery!

A quote:

- **"The life in front of you is more important than the life behind"**

My Important Injury

by Dalv

I wish I knew then what I know now. I could have taken a different perspective on my painful experience - a perspective I may have taken, although in hindsight I reject the idea as considering what I 'know' now is the result of my journey.

For me, the message that positivity can be taken from traumatic episodes seemed almost like there was consolation to look for. However, after actually living it, this concept was like those times you become aware of a new word, and you start hearing it all the time, like it has just come into existence. Now, sentiments like that of Fyodor Dostoevsky – that 'pain and suffering are always inevitable for a large intelligence and a deep heart' – ring true.

I don't actually remember how the initial injury occurred, which is somewhat surprising for something so significant, but consistent with the vague answer patients give when asked about the onset of their back pain. I suspect it was triggered by either an active sporting life or by taking on new, unpredictable physical loads in rehabilitation wards in my first year as an eager physio. What was clear is that its caned cut and it was not going away. A tearing sensation localised to the small of the back, frequent and irritated by movement, coupled with a disconcerting 'nervy' pulling in the right calf and buttock, an irritating tingling in the side of the foot. There was no doubt what was going on: a disc in my back had lost its integrity, and the nerve was being compromised. I knew it! Or maybe I 'knew' too much?

Working on a stroke unit as a physiotherapist meant using your body weight and strength to assist patients to move, often including walking soon after they had lost the ability to use limbs on one side of their body. This is to take advantage of the vital period of rewiring of the brain as it is repairing from being starved of oxygen. As I was aware that discs were often injured and overloaded through bending and lifting, which was consistent with what actually happened, I naturally compensated. I didn't allow my spine to bend, in order to protect it. Maybe more so due to my textbook knowledge. Being a 24-year-old male with a pride and ego to match, together with an appropriate sense of duty as a physiotherapist, I persevered through the pain – until the pain was so unbearable.

I realised I couldn't tolerate the pain anymore and felt like I was causing irreparable harm. This was heart-breaking for me since I've always been an active person. Even as a toddler, my childhood energy levels gave my parents the run around, and would often involve them having to apologise on my behalf, whilst trying to stop me from grabbing on to anything to climb, even unsuspecting strangers' hair. This continued through my fun-filled childhood years, where not a day would go by without me coming home battered from putting my body through the mill, using the neighbourhood as a giant playground. The activities varied, from kicking a ball around for 8 hours, using alleys as goals, to partaking in marathon long 'run out' sessions, as well as getting up to some early teenage mischievous pursuits. Looking back, that endurance seems almost superhuman, but at the time the cuts, bruises and sore muscles just felt like the norm. This physicality put me in good stead, helping me keep my head held high in a rough-around-the-edges west London school and neighbourhood, as well as being able to partake in kicking a ball around a field at a decent level. The confidence gained from this transferred into a busy and adventurous social life, travelling on a whim, making the most of my university years, enjoying the party scene and making new friends along the way. All in all, this was who I was, and it was all because of what my body was able to do.

After the injury, I had a few stints of work, altered duties and phased returns, little motivation to meet friends, or book a trip away, knowing my restricted movements would consume my thoughts. My identity appeared to be fading; this was my perspective. It's all I knew.

If I were to look at it from a different angle, with hindsight (and maybe analysing this chapter as I write it has allowed me clarity) I would say yeah, it was crap, but there were so many silver linings. The people in my life cared for me and supported me, particularly my mother, who worked in healthcare and gave sound advice, close friends who motivated me to get out of my head for a while and spend some time with them, and a girlfriend who was lovely and understanding. After an interesting and valuable (but at times gruelling) six-month stint working in the stroke unit, my rotation changed to a less heavy MSK department, where dealing with back pain and referred leg pain was a common patient presentation. The dynamics were beautifully unique, and I became good friends with my colleagues, who would offer help as they could see I was distressed on a daily basis. I received off-the-cuff treatment, manual therapy, acupuncture, suggested exercises to try and soft tissue release techniques, all be it quite ad hoc. I was grateful. Who knows what would have been different if I could have seen the positives? But my vision was impaired by a thick, grey cloud.

It was called 'chronic pain' then. Chronic pain is the terminology used when the problem lasts for longer than 3 months, as this is normally the time frame it takes for most tissue in the body to heal. There are a number of reasons someone may feel pain after this time, there can be physical, psychological and social reasons that keeps the pain persisting. They say there are links between being in a lower socio-economic group, lower health literacy or mental health problems and being more predisposed to have this 'persistent pain' presentation, the now more appropriately used phrase.

The population we served in North London contained a demographic with these associated characteristics. It must be said that it is most definitely not exclusive to these groups. The reason we had a department that looked how best to deliver assessment and management to those who suffered with persistent pain.

A consultant physio was the lead for the department where experienced clinicians, with the help of a psychologist, would often carry out the treatment for the more complex cases. A large majority of patients I would treat were 'chronic pain' patients, and I would refer the ones that I got very stuck with. After screening the patient to check that onward medical attention wasn't needed, I would encourage movement with exercise and explain the physiology and psychology relevant to their presentation, using the training I had and what I understood by it. I thought I understood it: 'The pain someone experiences doesn't equate to how much tissue is injured'; 'a scan won't change the course of treatment'; 'exercise releases hormones that reduce pain and improve mood, which can help to break the pain-inactivity-pain cycle'; 'massage is unlikely to help long term' were some of the things I would say.

Having had the problem for nearly a year now, I was playfully teased by my colleagues that I was a 'chronic pain patient'. I would chuckle a little, and tell them to 'piss off', not letting on that I felt hurt and insulted, as if I wasn't believed. I vividly recall my colleague Sarah, reporting to me that the pain clinical specialist had said 'He just needs to get his core muscles as strong as possible', like my problem wasn't going to get better, and I had to just 'manage it'.

I started to become bitter, almost resigned to the fact that my life wouldn't pan out how I had wanted it to. It consumed my thoughts. I was chasing solutions over the months: scans, private specialist physios. A lot of time residing in bed, withdrawing into myself. Not having a vent for my high energy translated into sadness and frustration.

The turning point wasn't anything epic. It was subtle, but vital. I was working on the wards again, not having had any treatment for a while. I was reluctant to ask physio friends for help. On reflection, probably because I was trying to avoid mixing this negative undertone that remained present in my consciousness with the invading warm moments of spending valuable time with my mates.

Now, in the main hospital building, one of my colleagues who worked in the MSK department, Leanne, offered to have a look at my back. It was too sincere an offer to refuse. Explaining to her where I was with it, she listened intently, apparently without judgment. Treatment was delivered with compassion, something I hadn't received throughout this struggle. Consistent with this tone, she encouraged me to move in the way I had been avoiding, that I had convinced myself was harmful. Gradually and slowly heeding this encouragement, a 'hard hitting' realisation struck me: it was the phrase, the labelling of being a 'chronic pain patient' which had bought me down. Putting everything into place, the road to my recovery had revealed itself.

I started to be able to execute the messages being repeated to those in a similar position and use it to understand my problem. 'A bad day doesn't mean you are back to square one', 'pain doesn't mean my body harm' and many other started to be truly lived and believed. I had to be conscious of my habitual reactions to the symptoms, my mood when I felt the pain, my muscles seizing up and the way I moved, so I could counter it. I quite often did this by taking deep breaths, which allowed me to be present, not constantly away with these thoughts. This new, helpful perspective was being validated.

At times I would ruminate on how I had wasted valuable time, hadn't progressed in my social life, sporting life or career, how I had spent so much time preoccupied, and was often short-tempered with those I loved. It was frustrating: I was my own worst enemy.

Luckily the turning point was when I saw the irony of the situation. I was not progressing with these regrets either. It was 'clear' that my ability to look at the thoughts – as an outsider – and analyse their ineffectiveness was catalysed by this experience. It punched the ego in the face and allowed my mind to open. I was grateful, to everything that had preceded the compassionate interaction I had, it all counted, everyone who had offered their help, all the support and love I had been shown, was the reason I wasn't still suffering.

The idea that I believed in – that being called a 'chronic pain patient' was an insult - showed how little I knew. My conceitedness got in the way, my refusal to acknowledge the truth because it challenged my beliefs. To be fair to me, this often comes with age. There are sayings such as 'young and stupid' and 'old and wise'. Not saying I am at all yet wise, and definitely not yet old! But it seems this humbling experience of keeping an open mind has allowed me to show the compassion I received back to those I am fortunate to care for. Some have suffered with pain for a lifetime, which puts this episode into perspective, but having an inkling of what they may be going through has put me in a better stead to help. Even if I am just a stepping stone, showing compassion.

In this story, I often put a word like 'knew' in inverted commas as these, appeared to be the barriers to my overcoming hurdles. I attempt to take this approach to all my relationships. Listening rather than providing all the answers to problems for friends, I seem to have gained the best friendships I have ever had. It seems you can be confident without giving the impression that you know everything. Not having this burden of needing all the answers allowed me to be less caught up in thought. I am more present; this itself is freeing of pain.

Physically, there is nothing I feel is out of my grasp. I boulder, practice yoga and Pilates most days, and say yes to any adventure involving a physical challenge. I doubted I would get here at one point. But now I know it was inevitable.

It was a long, windy road: the challenges were like trees which had fallen over needing to be dodged, with some poor orienteering skills leading me perhaps in random towns with dead-ends and have to reverse back out, but I eventually made it somewhere good. I know there is a long way to go still, and I have no desire for this journey to end.

- **'We age not by years, but by stories'**

Quote by Maza-Dohta

A New Path

Anonymous

As I pulled my jeans up my legs and towards my waist, I noticed a tension and wondered if these were my girlfriend's denims. I pulled the button and the clasp, took a deep breath and quickly shoved the two elements together hoping they'd do their job, lock in and let me breath out. They did, and as I relaxed and breathed out, I watched my belly expand and hang over my belt. "Looks like you're going to need bigger trousers" I thought, Again! I'd never been a very active person or worried about my weight before, but something had happened and needless to say I was in a rut.

For most of my life my mind had always been on cruise control. Not that I didn't think, I just didn't think about things in much detail. Go with the Flow. Easy like Sunday Morning. It was an easy way to be. Towards the latter part of my twenties, questions started coming into my teens "What are you doing with your life?", "Where are you going?", "Are you happy?". My family has always been a fairly typical English conservative family, where feelings and emotions were generally reserved and kept to yourself. Hell, I didn't even know what anxiety was until I was 29 and it's something I'd felt consistently throughout my life.

Later that day I was standing the top of my ladder at work, drilling holes into the steel bullet resistant security door I'd been working on. I wasn't happy. "What happened?" I thought, his plan had been to be a Hollywood Movie Director but I was standing on a bleak factory in Hertfordshire with a team of co-workers who resembled Dads Army crossed with the people from Wall-E. I'd wandered aimlessly down a road to what was feeling like a dead end and was suddenly wandering how I'd ended up here.

As I contemplated buying a new pair of trousers – a bigger pair of trousers, I thought "Something needs to change!". I was never great at sports as a kid and I've always been embarrassed to exercise because of it. That night, I grabbed my trainers, put on my shorts and decided to go for a run. The first run of my life. I set out a very short route (literally around the block), grabbed by black jumper, pulled my hood up and went for it. It was a freezing January evening, but the moment I started moving I could feel the heat quickly taking over my body. As I found my stride, I quickly hit my wall. My breathing got heavy, my legs began to ache and the cold in my lungs felt like shards of ice in my chest. I persisted and competed my route, returning home a sweaty mess and struggling for breath. I laid on my bed – my chest burning from the cold air in my lungs and I thought to myself, "I'm screwed".

I persisted with my plan and stuck to this run every day for a week. It wasn't a long route, but it was something and I'd stuck to it. With this new determination I set out a plan to run every day, starting small and upping the length a little more each week. I incorporated a weekly weigh in and when Friday came, I was genuinely excited to see if there had been a change. I stepped up to the scales and looked down to see I'd lost 4 pounds. "4 pounds? Is that a lot?". I thought about a pound bag of sugar, and then pictured four. "That's not bad!". Encouraged by this, I started to watch what I was eating more which wasn't too hard. I spent a lot of time travelling around in a White Van eating fast food, so making adjustments here and regular exercise soon started making a difference. The next week it was 4 pounds again. Then 5, then 8. The weight was falling off and I was feeling great. I can't help but look back now and hear the Rocky montage theme over the top of it. I was a man on a mission.

After 6 months of this new regime, I was feeling great. I was happier, healthier and more energised. But I still found myself standing at work at the top of that ladder, thinking "What happened?" I was unhappy and realising it wasn't just the weight but also the work. I'd never really considered being super happy with work – it's just work – a job. But the job I was in wasn't where I wanted to be. The dream had always been film or television, but I was 27, had no experience and living in Hertfordshire. It was going to be tough, but it was now or never.

I started by applying to some entry level jobs at small media companies and soon managed to get an interview with a little documentary company. I nervously got on the train to London trying to remember all the key phrases in my head; "I'm a trouble shooter", "I'm a go-getter", "I'm a team worker", "I'm hungry to work".

I was sitting the meeting room when a lady walked in with a lot of attitude and thick New York accent. "Why should I hire you then?" she asked bluntly.

"Well, I'm probably older than most of the applicants, but I'm starting a new path in my life, I'm determined, I have common sense….and I'm not going to take shit from people." I sounded more convincing than I expected. She smiled and the meeting continued well. I left confident and I was soon happy to get a call offering me the job.

The job was a tiring one. I soon found out my new bosses were newly ex husband and wife, and their patience for one another was very thin. I'd unknowingly suddenly become the son of two parents, passing notes between them as they argued for the company. Determined, I got my head down, got on with my new job and continued to learn from anyone I could. Any person we had come in, I would sit down and question about what they did and what they'd worked on. I wanted to know all about the industry and what my options were. I knew TV had a lot of different avenues, so I was keen to explore what there was, to try and to choose path with more thought this time.

One day, we had a new Producer come in to work on a new show the company had just commissioned. She was a smart dressed woman and carried herself with so much confidence. We started talking and I soon found out she'd just finished eight years working on a huge project, a documentary series for the BBC. She'd come up with the idea for the project herself, got it commissioned, produced it and then went on a national tour speaking about it. Her passion and love for what she did was very inspiring to me and it made me think that's what I want to do. I wasn't sure exactly what, but I knew I wanted to do it with passion.

I continued on my new path, eventually leaving that company and moving on to work at many different TV companies, being fortunate enough to work with the Premier League and travel around to most of the best stadiums abroad. I succeeded to progress in my role and moved up, soon managing shows and overseeing the general logistics of shoots. I've had the opportunity to work on some amazing shows and work with some of the most talented people in the industry.

I learned that no matter what, if you want anything in life you have to get up, do it yourself and stick to it. There will be help on the way and there will be ups and downs, but only you who can make anything happen.

The best memory I have was working on a sport event hosted in Botswana, Africa. For two weeks, I got to drive my crew around the most picturesque country I've ever seen and meet the kindest, most friendly people I've ever had the pleasure of meeting. On one of the days we were lucky to go on a Safari and as we were TV crew, we got to go extremely close to all the animals. I got to see lions, elephants, giraffes, zebra's and monkeys, all in their natural environment and it was for work!

We pulled over towards the end of the day to shoot some pieces on camera, and as the camera man set up, he asked me to grab a reflector shield and jump up a ladder to help the light. I grabbed the reflector from the bag, climbed up and looked out as the sun was going down over the African dessert. As I stood at the top of my ladder, I thought in amazement "What happened?".

I Andy

by David A Williams

I was adopted by a well-to-do kindly couple when I was just a baby, the couple had one daughter who was also adopted.

My adoptive parents were the only parents I knew, the fact that I was adopted was not kept a secret from me. The only thing I knew of my previous life was that my name was Steven Harris, I was born in Croydon in 1962.

The memories of my early childhood were happy, we lived in a lovely spacious 4-bedroom detached house in Maidenhead. I enjoyed going to school and loved my home. My father had to work away from home frequently, he worked very hard. My sister Cathy was older than me and we got on fairly well together. My mum and me were very close, I really loved my mum. My mum stayed at home and looked after us, I wanted for nothing.

My parents separated when I was eight years old, I first lived with my dad and sister. I remember feeling very confused, hurt and unwanted, I felt that my maternal mother had not wanted me and now my adoptive mother had left me.

I really missed my mum who had gone on to live in a council house on a council estate. Life was miserable without mum around and I found myself worrying about her being on her own.

My mum had left to live with a man she had fallen in love with, but soon he got cold feet and left her. As it was seen as a disgrace for women to leave their husbands in those days, most of my mum's family and friends were no longer in contact. Life was difficult for a single woman.

During the time I lived with my dad I was given a little part-time job by a family friend who appeared very friendly and fond of me, but one day he sexually abused me. I told my father and my perpetrator was arrested but it left me feeling very angry and bitter. I found it hard to trust people.

After a year with my father I made the decision to live with my mum on the council estate. Life was very hard for a child on the local estate, as it was in a poverty-stricken area. It was a rough area where there were gangs and burglaries, car theft, fights. Stabbings were a frequent occurrence. My mum was working in an office and was just about making ends meet. In my teenage years, I hated school, instead of going to school I started to play truant.

In order to defend myself on the rough streets I got involved in a car stealing gang and helped steal lots of cars. Due to the environment it was inevitable for me to get involved in drugs. At 15 I was caught and was charged for 98 offences of stealing. I was sentenced to 3 months, of which I served two weeks in prison and I was on bail and remanded for two years. During the period I was on bail I lived with my father who was supportive. Having realised the consequences of stealing, I stirred myself away from the gangs and decided I would never steal again.

At 17 I was a young punk in Maidenhead, one of my better past times was playing the guitar, I loved the guitar. I used to put on an act of being tough but it was just an act. I did not feel tough, I actually felt very insecure and lacking confidence. At this time, I was still taking drugs, on one occasion I took too much speed and acid and went off the rails and was extremely ill. My mum supported and nursed me back to health. I learnt a lot of life lessons.

I took on various jobs such as working in building sites, and at the same time I got into a band. I have had many nick names in my life but the nick name that really stuck with me as, 'Andy Guitar,' I became the main singer and guitarist. We did cover songs and sometimes I wrote and sang my own songs mainly in clubs.

Sadly, everyone in the music industry was taking drugs in those days. Even though we started to get very popular it did not last as I was taking too much LSD and speed. I went off my head and totally lost it, and had a near death experience. I can relate to people who talk about outer body experiences, as I also had an outer body experience. Amazingly I survived due to my mum's love and care, and once again I remained in my mum's home till, I fully recovered.

I met a girl at 23 who was besotted by me, I think she loved the fact that I was a musician. She became pregnant and, doing the right thing I married her. I have a strong moral that you should treat people as you would want them to treat you. Even though I did not love her I felt that I should do the right thing and marry her. Sadly, the marriage did not last, and my wife had custody of my daughter

I kept in contact with my daughter till she was 11 when my ex-wife took her away after which my daughter has never been the same with me.

Following the failure of my first marriage, I gave up drugs for many years. Over the years I married twice in total and had 2 steady relationships. I have five children in total, all my children are now grown up and leading their own life.

I have succeeded in giving up drugs several times over the years, the longest period that I was drug free was 6years. My mother who had been my main social support and the center of my life died 6 years ago.

That time things were looking great and everything was going my way. I had a fairly good relationship with my children, I owned a property and had started a business which was thriving. I did not grieve for my mother as I felt she was still around, I made myself believe she was still alive.

But 3 years ago, I had a nervous breakdown, I felt very depressed. Reality had hit me that I would never see my mother again and I started grieving. I felt shattered and could not cope with daily life, I fell back to taking drugs and lost everything I had built over the years. I lost my business, became bankrupt, I did not have a penny to my name, I started living on the streets. My children distanced themselves from me and we lost all communication.

Life was not good on the streets, I was sleeping in doorways and awakened and being ushered away at dawn. Initially I did not care, I felt like a victim but I have an inner strength which came to the surface on many occasions. I said to myself: that's enough

Andy. 2 years ago, I picked myself up and went to the GP's for help and have been on methadone ever since.

Since my near-death experience at 19, my faith in the spiritual being have been strong. In spite of my lifestyle I have compassion for those around me. The first person I helped to come clean from drugs was 20 years ago, and he is living a normal life drug-free even today. Over the years I have successfully helped 8 people give up drug addiction. I feel that is what my goal in life has been.

Over the three years on the streets I have played my guitar and sang to earn money. Sometimes I work many hours. There are people who look down on a homeless guy living on the streets. But it is amazing how many people will bring me food, drink and clothes. People in Maidenhead often stop to talk to me. I have made many friends in Maidenhead, and I look after my friends. I have a friend at present that I look out for and he is taking methadone like me. I have now been clean from drugs for two years. The council have put me up in temporary accommodation's in Bray just before Christmas 19.

It is not easy coming off drugs. The symptoms you get are pain, irritability, insomnia. The only thing that can keep you going is knowing there is light at the end of the tunnel. When I help those, who want to give up drugs I drum it in their heads that it is worth going through the agonizing symptoms and after a few weeks they will see light again through the darkness. Of course, when helping others through rehabilitation you need to be on call day and night. Often people think that cannabis is a drug which is not addictive and is safe to take, what they don't realize is that it is actually a gateway to other drugs.

People on the streets may see me as a loser, but I see myself as a fighter who does care about others. One of the skills I gained through the better years when I did not take drugs was of a counselor. My future hope is not to forget the despair of the process of giving up drugs as I have done in the past, to take myself off methadone and to help others from destroying themselves.

Each day I wonder how I am alive when I have abused my body so much, surely there is a purpose!

My Story as an HCM Carrier
by Inderdeep Birk

In life there are many genetic disorders, my story of such a genetic disorder is called Hypertrophic cardiomyopathy (HCM). HCM is an inherited condition that can cause the heart muscle to thicken and become stiff, making it harder for it to pump blood. I was only aware I was the carrier of this gene at the age of 43.

I had passed down a gene for a heart condition I didn't know I had; it was devastating. I couldn't believe it when I heard the words: 'You're the carrier.' We found out after Maninder (my son from my first marriage) became unwell on his 16th birthday. He had played rugby at school and spent the day with friends celebrating his birthday. When he came back to our home that evening, he said he felt heavy in the chest. I gave him indigestion tablets and he went to bed. Around midnight he came into our bedroom and said he didn't feel good at all. While he was talking to me, he said he had no energy and just dropped onto the bed. I took him straight to A&E and stayed with him overnight, surrounded by heart monitors. He was so scared. When my son became unwell, I never expected to discover an inherited heart condition that would change the life of the whole family.

In the morning, the doctor came and spoke with my husband Balwinder and me. She said Maninder had a heart condition called hypertrophic cardiomyopathy, but they didn't know the severity yet. We were transferred to the Royal Brompton Hospital under the care of Dr Sanjay Prasad. He told us that Maninder's condition could be looked after with a low dose of beta blockers and regular check-ups. But then came the biggest blow. Dr Prasad told Maninder he was going to have to make big changes. Sports like rugby were too risky now – he would have to stop playing. This devastated him. Within days he had gone from being asked to join Bath University's rugby team, to being told not to lift heavy objects or run for a bus. He was so angry and just kept saying: 'Why me?' Dr Prasad also told us about HCM being an inherited condition. I was given a blood test and it confirmed I was the carrier of the faulty gene.

I was devastated when we found out my younger son Manny had it too. Very quickly, I started to experience symptoms. I was breathless and had problems climbing the stairs. Some mornings I was so dizzy I couldn't get out of bed. We all had regular checkups.

In 2011, Dr Prasad reviewed me. He put me on medication and told me I would need an ICD, which also has a pacemaker function. After these treatments I felt better straight away, but soon the palpitations & dizziness returned, I had several Ablations. I started having good days when I would be up and step out of the house and days bed-bound.

In September 2017 I was put on the urgent heart transplant list. This came as a complete shock. But I was told everything was in my favour, as my other organs are healthy. I knew this was my only chance, but before I made the decision, I sat down with Balwinder and my two boys to talk honestly about how they felt. It has been a lot to digest, but my sons told me: 'We don't just want you for the short term, mum. We want you for the long term.' I am blessed to have such a supportive family.

I didn't have to wait for long – I had a heart transplant on 4th of October. The doctors said my new heart was slow to start, and my recovery has been slow too. I still go for regular checks-ups at the hospital, taking each day as it comes. I am remaining very hopeful. Having undergone surgery, I realized there were others who had similar problems but could not go through surgery for various reasons, one of the reasons is not having a compactible donor. I realized that I was indeed very fortunate.

Both my sons also have their own story to tell of the time after they were diagnosed.

My older son Maninder who was 16 at the time, hearing that he couldn't play rugby any more was one of the hardest things for him to cope with. He was captain of the rugby team at the time, and was about to go on tour in Wales. Rugby was his main love in life. He went through various emotions, he was angry and frustrated at times, sometimes he appeared as if he did not care. I was worried about him but one day he came home with a positive outlook and made changes in his life to adapt to his condition. Instead of playing rugby he got into rugby coaching and started playing cricket. He still showed determination and pushed himself, but he learnt the limits between doing exercise and keeping safe. He says he feels extremely lucky as he is able to lead a normal life and is at present stable. Maninder keeps busy and is currently working at a large car rental firm. He shows a great deal of concern for me and his brother and is so caring.

My younger son Manvir (Manny) was monitored regularly ever since he was 9 years old. He showed traces of the gene when he was 11, He had an ablation and ICD implant when he was 15yrs old. He was really scared, as I had been through it all. I was able to help calm him down; I did my best to reassure him. His energy levels are still very low, he has suffered from palpitations and dizziness and had Ablations in 2012. So understandably, it has made going to school and having a normal social life difficult for a teenager. He hasn't been able to do a full week at school, and have had to be home-schooled. I am so proud of him as he has been so positive through it all. He lives his life as fully as he can within his limits. He has now started at college studying business studies. When he finishes college, he wants a career in human resources.

During the difficult time when I was going for a transplant, we were counselled from the British Heart Foundation (BHF). They introduced me to one of the members who already had a Transplant, so was helpful talking through all the things I needed to know and spoke to my family during my post-Transplant recovery. Although I have never met him, as we only chatted on the phone, he helped us understand, the 'what, why and how's'. He was one of our saviors as he supported us through the time when we were ignorant of what was happening to us and how to move on, he was on the phone every day and whenever we needed to talk to him. He made things clear to us until we felt we could cope with what was happening in our lives.

We as a family have shared all our trials and tribulation, I feel we are stronger and closer as a family and extremely lucky. I have been interviewed on various occasions both in the journal and Television, it is mainly because by sharing our story we may help others to understand and realize there is still hope and move on to lead a fulfilling life.

Maninder and Manvir would one day like to have a family of their own and know that the condition could be passed down. This is where research could help play a part. It is a Boost to know that BHF is helping to explore this. We are all optimistic that very soon something could make things easier.

The Wheels of Life Through Her Eyes

Anonymous

Are parents right when they do their best? Is their love in the protection they show you? The type of protection where you have been lucky to be allowed to go to your best friend's party but a restricted time have been given to return home. To top it all the party is in her family home and you are the only guest at the party, so when you leave the party is over.

Their idea of your childhood was to entertain yourself in a family; walking to the library or school was the most freedom you achieved.

Her parents did not trust the country we were invited to live in. One of her father's saying was 'don't forget your roots, cause the English will throw us out of the country…'! It was obvious that was what many patriots would have liked, to throw the coloured immigrants out of the country. They wore different clothes, spoke a different language, ate different foods which smelled foul and tasted disgusting to some. But even if they were dressed in the European fashion and smelled of roast dinners, they were easy to identify but hard to mingle with. Their culture was way apart, absolutely strange and wrong! With such a difference how do they blend and be embraced in an English land?

Was it right inviting your father who had been called out to participate in the war to be employed in a country where they needed those dirty, trivial and manual jobs done? Let's face it: England in the 60's needed hard workers. And we were those hard workers!

Were the people right in calling you names when you were walking on the streets? A child starting senior school, where white children did not want to sit next to a coloured girl. It was better they stayed away from her than be abusive. To avoid abuse the children with the same skin colour formed a group. They played with their own kind; they understood their own kind. There were teachers who were kind and there were teachers who were hostile to a coloured child, even as a child she noticed and was saddened.

Such as the teacher who threw a bag of sugar on her head as she had been mischievous in the cookery class. She remembered the tears that poured down her face, she was a proud child and rarely ever cried in the presence of others, she could not talk of the incident. The name stayed as a memory, how could she forget the names or faces of the people who had an impact on you, no matter good or bad! Prejudices can be classified as ignorance, laughed at and forgotten, or the growing monster a lasting effect of hurt and tears, when playing at its worst can be the cause of bloodshed. Shadows never to be forgotten such as 'Blair Peach' the teacher from New Zealand who became a pillar of strength when he stood up against anti-racism and died in a demonstration in 1979, he never lived to tell the tale but a school was built to mark his name.

Even against her parent's strong advice such a child grew up to become a nurse, she became a nurse because she saw it as a vocation. It was something she had to do, there was no alternative. Where does this need came from? It was that love for people where she needed to care for others. She believed that people were mainly good.

The cultural teachings were strong, how do you defy parents when they say they are right and you grew up thinking they were right. They only did their best for you. They were not alone in their thinking; culture has the biggest impact where you think yours is the only way to live. Pride and dignity play a big part in being dogmatic against change. Parents have their own agendas. She wanted to be friends with the local people, but how could two worlds get on, when one thought they were superior and the other thought they were corrupted and ethically unjust. In every race there are people prejudiced against something or someone, but there are so many people who also try to fight prejudices and reach a world of 'Just'. But there are also those who are in constant battle of wanting power and control, not aware they are not in control, that the materialistic world is controlling them. They are constantly hungry always wanting more, greed causes constant fear about the rise of the struggling class. Will it mean there will be less for them and their loved ones? Feeling threatened by change! Just how much do they need to reach contentment!

Were her parents right to arrange her marriage to someone who was a stranger to her? They thought they were right otherwise they would not have done what they did. She knew they loved her; she knew they loved them all. This girl although not without faults was young and obedient enough to marry a man who was in the same cultural category as her parents. Only he had a temper, unlike her parents who in spite of their beliefs were kind people.

She was a girl who found things funny, who had a sense of humour. It did not help. He thought life had been unjust to him and violence was his right. Drinking gave him the excuse that, 'it wasn't him, it was the drink'. But the fact was he could not control his temper even when he was sober! She had a hard time with him mainly at night after his binge drinking. She persevered, as untangling a marriage needed a certain skill and divorcing was a taboo. Not wanting to shame and degrade the family, she hung on and every time she left him, she was persuaded to go back to. He would not leave her, he said he could not live without her.

Life was not bad all of the twenty-four hours a day, she was no longer a girl, she was now a woman. In the day she enjoyed bringing up her children and working, her children were the most wonderful thing that had happened to her. While bringing up her children she worked hard, ignoring exhaustion she did her best. She could enjoy herself with family friends and take her children on short holidays. She made the most of what she could. When people saw her, they thought she was happy. In actual fact, part of her life was happy, she had many memorable times. She made the most of the good times but often feared the bad nights, his moods were very changeable, the trigger could be anything or nothing.

When her mother had a stroke, she found it harder to smile, and after her death the silver lining on the clouds disappeared for a long time. After ten years of an abusive marriage she became stronger and knew she would leave him when the children were older. Violence had now become much less as she stood up to him much more. As she became stronger, he became weaker, a bully losses power and control at some time in his life and that causes self-destruction. Over a long period, alcohol can bring you down and weaken you permanently, friend becomes foe. A habit hard to break. She became brave, but the psychological trauma did tell its toil. Her children grew up and were now teenagers, they felt that their childhood was the best time of their lives. Did they feel the stability children should?

One day the time came when he fell off the stool when eating his dinner. Finally, on that day she knew she would stay with him no longer. The children were happy for her to move on. She walked out on him for good, she remembers that day, she found it so easy to go. He searched for her, he wanted her back. But she was gone, the children felt pity for him as he was now the victim and they attempted to change him, but very soon felt it was a lost cause, they followed her into a new life. At least they tried to build a bond, showing that family cared.

Compassion is a strange thing, sometimes we have more compassion for those who have been perpetrators instead of those whom have been hurt. It is all about how intense we portray our emotions, the person that cries and acts the victim the loudest get heard a lot easier. Pain is not seen when a person smiles and says she is fine. But it doesn't matter because when she smiles and says she is fine, then there comes a day when she is fine. Change is never easy, it comes with its tribulations, but tribulations are just hurdling and hurdles are not permanent if you learn that jump.

It felt like moving out of rainy winter days where everything is dull and lifeless towards the end of spring, where flowers have sprung up with many different colours and the air is ecstatic with sweet sounds and warmth. She simply settled to pursue her career and attempted to love and care for others. And as her children became recognized adults in society, she gave them the right to their own life choices, hoping their education and intelligence would enable them to rise above the muddy ground defining right from wrong. They say beauty is in the eye of the beholder, we choose what want to see and we see what we want to perceive.

Life change, generations change, lessons learnt by many embittered people. How many people mellow, become less ignorant and more tolerant as we get to that golden age here wisdom is the goal? Her children have grown to being broadminded men and are friends with all races, the gap between cultures can close with the right education. There are now a majority of people around her who have become closer to understanding and enjoying variety in cultures, different foods, clothing and arts. Those people intermingle readily, embracing and accepting. Let's face it the world, is constantly changing, we are all spinning on the wheel of life from which we jump off at different times on reaching our destination. Nothing has belonged to anyone, everything is borrowed. We are all guests in this world! Sometimes things seem unfair but in reflection are challenges a way of opening the doors to your inner resources and strength, for you to become that role model who can influence the wrongs in the world.

Dev

by Rajan Gujral

Dev was very happy today. He was so excited to receive a letter from his uncle to join him in his family business in Rangoon, Burma.

Dev had graduated from Punjab University, Jalandhar, in1937 and for the past three years he was training to be an accountant. This new opportunity, although more than 2700 kilometres from his hometown, seemed very attractive although a bit challenging.

He was always up for a challenge and decided to join his uncle in Burma [Now Myanmar] He travelled by road to Delhi and boarded a train for Calcutta, from there on he changed many coaches and almost took a week to reach Rangoon. His uncle, who was getting long in his tooth, was pleased to see Dev and introduced him to his teenage son Onkar.

Where two Rice Mills owned by Dev's Uncle, which he had inherited from his father [Dev's Grandfather], were to be managed by Dev. He was supposed to run the Rice Mills and at the same time train his Cousin in the business. It was his Uncle's wish that after his retirement both Dev and his Cousin will inherit a Mill each.

Dev was a fast learner and in no time not only did he learn the ropes of the Rice Mill business but within one year delivered a good return in the Business. Things were going so well that he was thinking of asking his father and sister to migrate to Rangoon.

Before the Second World War broke out Burma was part of The British Empire having been progressively occupied and annexed following three Anglo-Burmese wars in the 19th century. Burma became a separate colony under the Government of India Act 1935. Under British Rule substantial economic development of Burma took place. The local Bamar Community was increasingly getting concerned about the importation of Indian professionals and workers for many of the new industries.

In December 1942, Dave was planning to travel back to Lahore and bring his father and Sister back to Burma for permanent settlement. He was still planning the logistics of his travels when the news broke out of the Invasion of Burma by the Japanese Army. Japanese invasion of Burma was the opening chapter of the Burma Campaign in the South-East Asian Theatre of World War-2 and thus began the occupation of Burma.

Japanese Army was ruthless in its campaign. Rangoon was initially defended relatively successfully against Japanese air raids. In January 1942, the main body of the Japanese 55th Division began the main attack Westwards from Rahaeng in Thailand across the Kawkareik Pass. The Army guarding this approach retreated hastily westwards. The advancing Japanese army shot anyone in its way. Dev, along with his cousin and elderly uncle, left everything as it is and grabbed whatever they could and ran westwards.

They were on the run for about ten days when his uncle breathed his last. There was no time for his funeral as they had to stay ahead of the advancing Japanese army.

During the day, whenever they heard the sound of aeroplanes, they had to hide under bushes or in the paddy fields under water using straws to breathe. They had no option but to keep moving on foot, eating whatever they could get their hands on and drinking water from the rice fields. They had lost count of the days, on the run along with hundreds of other civilians in similar situation. It was nothing short of a miracle when they reached a refugee camp on the Indian Border. From there it took another month for them to reach back to Lahore. One can only imagine the happiness of his father and sister when they showed up at home.

It took another five years for Dev to pick up all his strength to establish a new business in Lahore. His cousin Onkar went to settle in his wife's village in Orisa, South India. Dev got married in Lahore and was busy expanding his business interests.

At the stroke of midnight, on 15th August 1947, India and Pakistan gained their independence and became dominions within the British Commonwealth. Astonishingly, millions of people had no idea at the moment of freedom whether they were in India or

Pakistan as the boundary lines in the provinces of Bengal and Punjab had not yet been made public. This uncertainty aggravated the chaos and panic. Sir Cyril Radcliffe, a British Lawyer, tasked with demarcating the boundary line, had never previously been to India and was given a mere forty days to decide on the border.

He spent much of his time in the confines of the Viceroy's House in Delhi. He did not once visit the actual areas or communities he was dividing.

The border was announced on 17th August 1947, it is believed that Radcliffe wrote to his stepson that no one in India would love me for what I have done. Millions of people will be looking for me and I do not want them to find me. Evidently when he came back to England, he burnt all his papers related to the partition.

Dev found himself on the wrong side of the Border as Lahore [then Capital of Punjab] was awarded to Pakistan. Unthinkable Violence erupted. Once again Dev had to drop everything he had owned or knew and started his march along with his father, wife and young Son from Lahore [Now in Pakistan] towards India on foot.

This mass migration coupled with terrible violence or the perceived threat of violence was the largest single movement of people outside of war or famine in human history. It is estimated that between 10 to 12 million people migrated during partition and majority of them were from Punjab. Millions were on the move. Safety was only in numbers. People marched together in large groups with children, women and elderly in the middle and men on the outside with whatever weapons they could lay their hands-on like Sticks, swords or metal bars. Even these large groups were faced with violent attacks by the opposite sides. There was no time to bury or cremate the dead. It is estimated that two million people died in this bloody mass migration.

After four days of this torturous Journey the lucky survivors arrived at the Indian Boarder. They were very weak and starving. The Indian Army took them to Refugee camps. They were given some food and water. After months of filling forms, Dev was allocated a mud house in Jalandhar. Before he could move into this mud house his wife passed away from the stress and illness she caught en route.

Once again Dev had to pick up the pieces and rebuild his life.

His experience in the running of a Rice Mill and accounting degree got him a job as an ordinary clerk within Food Corporation of India. Dev remarried in 1948. Dev was thankful that he had survived two horrendous catastrophes in human history. Dev put all his effort in re-rebuilding his life. He studied in the evenings and sat for internal departmental exams and worked his way up from being an ordinary clerk in the Food Corporation of India to one of the highest in office in his department as The General Manager of Super Bazaars of Government of Punjab.

Dev retired in 1973, his hard work had assured him a good pension, comfortable savings and many Assets to live a comfortable retired life.

Dev's daughter had qualified as a Doctor and had emigrated to New Orleans in USA. She invited her parents to visit her. This was Dev's first trip abroad after his life in Burma. He loved New Orleans and expressed his desire to settle in New Orleans. Although Dev's wife was in agreement, she did not wish to sell their two houses in India, which were being inhabited by their two sons and their families.

America was no place for a pensioner to start work and settle without massive financial injection. He assured his wife that he will not sell his assets in India but will start afresh in USA. This presented a huge challenge. But Dev always relished a challenge.

Within a month he secured a job as a book keeper in a small factory and rented a flat. Dev applied for a licence to practice as an accountant. The authorities in New Orleans refused to acknowledge his Accounts Degree from India.

Undeterred at age 69, he joined an evening college and studied for two years to obtain his American Accounts Degree and Licence to Practice within the State of Louisiana.

Soon Dev was running his successful Accountant Practice and worked for a further 30 years. He was still practicing when he stepped into the hundredth year of his life. After a brief illness he breathed his last on 25th June 1917. He was survived by his daughter and two sons, 9 grandchildren and 17 great grandchildren

Dev, my Dad led an exemplary life. He had known defeat but never got defeated, known loss but found his way out.

My father had a very simple view of life; you don't get anything for nothing. Everything has to be earned, through work, persistence and honesty.

Over the years I watched my Dad help so many people less fortunate than him. Whenever my mum would appoint a live-in home help, he would start teaching them basic reading and writing or some basic skill like driving and helping them to get jobs such as a driver or a peon to the great annoyance of mum. She would say that she has taken so much time and effort to train them and now they were gone. He always told her that 'They are now in a more secure and pensionable job with better life prospect'.

I watched him work hard not only to improve his life. He always helped and encouraged others less fortunate than him to improve their lot.

He would always remind us of the following life principles: -

- "A man can do what a man has done".

- "A stich in time saves nine".

- "You never fail unless you stop trying".

- "Age is a matter of Mind and if you do not Mind it does

   not matter"

And finally

- "Do Good and Forget".

When I was an evacuee

by Stella Clothier

In the summer of 1940, after Dunkirk, it was decided to evacuate the town children to the safety of the countryside away from the bombing and the threat of invasion by the German army. I was then a pupil at Deanery School for girls in Southampton and most of us were evacuated to Castle Cary. We travelled by train from Southampton Central Station and although our parents were asked not to come to the station lots of them did.

Most of us were very excited, but there were quite a few tears as well, and as we travelled along things got quieter and quieter. This was not just a day out in the country, it could be for a very long time and as it turned out in my case for the rest of my life.

We all had labels attached to our clothes and we were only allowed to take one small suitcase with a change of clothing and of course gas masks in their little cardboard boxes and our identity cards. I still have mine and my number was ECAD44/8.

When we arrived at Wincanton, we were taken by bus to Castle Cary to the Old School in the town and from there by car to our new homes by Miss Mary Mackie who later arranged for us to join the Girl Guides.

I and another girl were billeted with Mr. Walter Martin and his housekeeper Miss Gibson at Torbay House. It was a lovely old farmhouse but it had no electricity and the rooms were lit by beautiful oil lamps. Mr. Martin kept a few cows and some chickens and I loved to watch the cows being hand milked by Mr. Hayward who worked on the farm. Sometimes I helped collect the eggs. Mr. Martin did not have a car – he had something much better, a pony and trap and he would sometimes take me for a ride, and occasionally I was allowed to drive it around the field.

The new school at Ansford was not quite finished and our teachers took us for long walks when we picked blackberries and rosehips. We started school in September, Mr. Gough was the headmaster and Miss King headmistress. Digs Parslow, Miss

Blackmore, Mr. Spens, Mr. Strickland and Mr. Charlton were our Southampton teachers, and I was in class 3A with Mr. Charlton. The school was divided into four 'houses' Cranmore, Butleigh, Tor and Stourton. I was elected games captain for Cranmore, also a prefect and later head girl. All the local children came to the new school as well, but the infants and juniors had their own headmaster, Mr. Gomm.

In 1941 my home in Southampton was bombed and my mother came down to Castle Cary and stayed with Mrs. Fox in North Street until my dad managed to find another house on the outskirts of Southampton and she went home again. It was lovely having her and I missed her very much when she left. Unfortunately, Mr. Martin died and we girls had to move on.

By now the town was full with evacuees and the wives of soldiers, I eventually went to stay with Mr. and Mrs. Derrett at Abbey Gardens. He was a butcher with a shop in Fore Street and Mrs. Derrett worked in the office of Woodforde and Drewett solicitors. It was through her that I too went to work there.

Firstly, I went after school and Saturday mornings for which I was paid 3s 6d until I left school at 15, and then worked full time for 7s 6d a week. I had shorthand lessons from Mr. Chilcott until he was called up. Mrs Derrett had to go to hospital and I was on the move again. This time I went to stay with Mr. and Mrs. Bush and my friend Marjorie, until in 1944 I returned home.

I worked in another legal office but it was mainly court work which I did not like. I stayed there for a year but when I was offered my old job back with Mr. Drewett, I returned to Castle Cary and lodged with Mr. and Mrs. Bush again. So now I was no longer an evacuee – I was a lodger.

In 1950 I married Edwin Clothier whose family has lived in Castle Cary for several generations. For the first year we lived with Ed's parents until we moved to 8 Park Avenue, I was still working with Mr. Drewett and Ed was working at Cary Station. We had two daughters, Sally and Barbara and when I was asked to go back to the office part time, Ed's mum looked after the girls.

In 1965 we bought a newsagent business from our friend Hetty Barber and we moved to the shop in Fore Street now occupied by

Palmer and Snell. Of course, I had to stop work but it did mean I was at home all day for the girls. Ed by then was working in Yeovil, but he helped me with the papers in the morning, while I ran the shop. It was very hard work and the hours were long giving us little free time to ourselves, but I had two very good assistants, Joan Sweet and Joyce Close.

Both our girls were married in 1976 and we decided to sell the shop and went to live in a house we had built in the Park. Ed took early retirement and became a gardener; I went back to the office yet again. By then I had worked for three generations of the Drewett family, R.B. Drewett, R.J Drewett and John Drewett. I retired in 1991 and at first was utterly lost – I just did not know how to fill my days. However, I belonged to the Young Wives and W.I. of which I have been a member for 54 years. I also helped with the teas when the Cricket Team played at home; enjoyed knitting, reading, cooking, walking with Ed and time with my family.

In 2010 we celebrated our diamond wedding and had a lovely lunch at Holbrook House for our family and friends, and our girls took us on a trip on the Orient Express, which was a wonderful experience. We now have 6 grandchildren and 5 great grandchildren. Mine has not been a very eventful life, but it has been a wonderfully happy one and I am grateful to everyone who helped to make it so.

A note from Sally:

My Mum wrote her story in 2012, when she was 87. She often spoke about being an evacuee, always positively, with lots of happy memories. I do remember when she bought ornaments of an evacuee girl and boy and set them in her display cabinet, each with their own small suitcase, name label on their coats and the girl was holding a Teddy Bear. She said "that little girl is just like me, except I didn't have a Teddy". This made me think about how difficult it must have been for Mum to leave her family – Mum, Dad, brothers and sisters, she was the youngest of 8, the city she had grown up in; her friends, school and everything familiar to her.

She was taken to a small country town 60 miles away; no distance today, but a long distance then; when transportation links were not as they are now, no mobile phones or social media communication …… just the good old British Mail, which transported and delivered those very important letters to and from her parents and family.

Mum thought herself very lucky and always said she was treated with love and kindness, but all the same her world was turned upside down with a complete change in lifestyle and location, living with families she had never met.

We can compare slightly the recent changes in our lifestyles as we live through a pandemic, lock down and negotiate the COVID-19 virus, but we do have advanced technology and many of us have been able to speak with our loved ones through the power of social media.

I believe my Mum's generation was strong and resilient. My Mum certainly made the absolute best of all she had and seized every opportunity – despite thinking her life was not very eventful.

She was an amazing role model to me, my sister, her grand-children and great grand-children until she passed away in 2018 aged 91.

Open Your Eyes, Open Your Heart & Let It Go!

Hardish Deol

We were a close-knit family and one of the highlights of my life was when I first saw the faces of my children after birth. I welcomed my daughters-in-law to the family and treated them like the daughters I never had. To have grandchildren bought me great joy, it was as if my family was completed.

Suddenly, a time of darkness dawned on us. I had to take my daughter-in-law to the police station. We were informed that the police wanted to have an informal chat with her. Five hours later we were informed that she was being charged with the manslaughter of her own baby daughter! The shock, anger and despair felt overwhelming. We could not believe this was happening.

Three years back, the memories of grief and anguish came flooding back to the day when our baby granddaughter passed away. Our miracle baby born at only twenty-five weeks was such a fighter. I always referred to her as my warrior princess. She had survived all odds and after four months in hospital came home. After only six weeks at home, she tragically passed away. The shock and disbelief of what happened was too much to bear. I cannot put into words that feeling of losing your grandchild. Just imagine only ten days later to have the finger of suspicion pointed at your children for their child's death!

The next three years was a living nightmare. My two little grandsons were taken away from their parents and I had to step in to take legal responsibility for them. There was a continuous assessment and involvement by social workers.

Had we as a family not suffered enough that now we had to deal with this charge on our daughter-in-law? We all felt numb with shock. Then we had to suffer what seemed like the longest wait for the trial to start. One long year of waiting anxiously and filled with anguish, it certainly took its toll on my family's health emotionally and mentally. So how do you prepare yourself?

The day of the trial arrived with everyone's nerves frayed. We did not know what to expect and our emotions were in turmoil. I did not know how to reach out to my daughter-in-law. She was an emotional wreck. We were all terrified of what the outcome might be. My faith was tested to the limit and at times during the trial everything seemed hopeless. But it was only my faith and true support of close family and friends that got us through this terrible time.

During the trial, sitting there listening to the prosecution saying terrible things about my family was very traumatic. Knowing that my daughter-in-law's life was in the hands of twelve jury members was very stressful. Would they see the genuine, kind and gentle woman that she is? I kept praying that the truth would prevail.

As the trial progressed, everything seemed to get more and more hopeless. The evidence was so twisted and having a judge that seemed biased against the defence did not help. The three weeks of the trial were filled with tears, terror and sadness.

When the trial concluded, the jury went out to deliver the verdict. At that point, we as a family were completely broken. We feared the worst as we were informed that the jury needed to give a unanimous verdict either for or against my daughter-in-law. Fearing that all odds were stacked against us, the wait for the verdict was unbearable. We had been informed that the jury could take days or weeks to reach a verdict. Just imagine the shock and surprise when we were informed the jury had come back with a verdict just hours later.

As we returned to the court room, we held our breath for those moments while trying to read the faces of the jurors.

The verdict of NOT GUILTY! did not register for a few seconds. Then the tears and overwhelming emotions just poured out, as I couldn't believe the fact that all twelve jurors believed my daughter-in-law to be innocent. They did not get swayed with all the lies of the prosecution. Justice did prevail and now we needed to move on with our lives. My prayers and faith kept me going and got us through this dark time.

Thinking back now, I reflect on people saying that everything happens for a reason. At the time, I was too hurt and angry to accept this.

In her short life, my baby granddaughter taught us powerful lessons. Our family values were tested. Our tolerance of each other was tested. We had to prevail against the dark times and accept her fate.

We granted everything that you are given and you want more and more. When something as precious as life is taken away you are left feeling so angry. I have now learned never to take anything for granted. Never to lose sight of the fact that nothing is yours.

I believe my granddaughter had links to our family from a previous life. My granddaughter's life would have been different to other children had she lived as she was deaf. Had she still been alive, I know our lives would have changed to adapt around her needs, but I miss the joy she would have brought. I often picture her in my… mind – ho-w she would have been now at four and half years old and wonder what we would have learned from her.

Looking to the future I hope to gain more strength from my experiences and I hope that by me sharing my story I have helped any reader that has struggled with loss of a loved one.

Rage

by Anabelle Zaychenko

I think back to the hard times and felt it couldn't have got any worse! In order to keep strong, I reassure myself by saying 'you know that things can't get any worse'! We can't compare with the life of others; we just have to make the best of our circumstances.

I had tried to commit suicide. It was when life was so difficult, there had been one thing after another knocking me down. I am so happy to be alive today!

I remember those happy days when I was a kid growing up in Russia. My dad had left my mum when she was pregnant with me, he never wanted any children. My mum was a strong capable career woman with many skills, she did her best for me as a single parent. Over the years she explored my talents, to see what I would excel in. I went to a sports school in addition to my normal schooling and an art school in the evening where I learnt music, art and dance. There was never a dull moment, I idolised my grandparents, I used to help my grandmother plant flowers, it was so therapeutic. My grandfather was a quiet, calm strict man and gave me lots of love, but recently told me all about his amazing life and the time he was in the army. My ideal man is based on my grandfather who I see as a role model of what a man should be. A man in my opinion should be devoted to his family, strict, fair and give lots of love and support, and be a good worker and provider. My uncle was like the brother I never had. We would chat and argue, but never held a grudge. I smile when I remember his sarcastic sense of humour, he was such a character, he did make me laugh.

I did not miss having a dad and only felt his loss when I was bullied at school. As in my early school days in Russia every normal family had a dad, you were looked down on if you did not have one. But I did not let that get me down, although my mother said that once I went up to a family with children and asked the man if he was my dad. But I can't remember it bothering me, not having a dad, as I had a grandfather and uncle and my life was happy and I felt it was complete.

Then came the change that led me to question the choices my mother had made. I was ten when my mother married an English man, he bought us over to live in England. It was a very abrupt change for a child, my mum and me had to adapt to a different culture, different language, but I wasn't fazed; I felt I could control the outcome. Maybe it was the competitiveness in sports. I viewed challenges as discovering the type of person you were and the type of person you could be. The lesson I learnt through being an active participant in sports was to never give up, undertaking challenges became a normal part of life.

There was harmony at home for about six months to a year but after that there were constant argument. My stepdad was mentally and physically abusive very often to my mother and sometimes to me. On one occasion, when I was a teenager, I was ironing, I could hear my stepdad being verbally abusive to my mother. Something in me snapped, I experienced a rage building up in me, I took the iron and threw it at him, it narrowly missed him. That did frighten him, he became ever so wary of me after that. We moved out soon after that incident, my mum rented a very small one-bedroom flat, there was asbestos in the bedroom. Although a dingy flat, it was a place of safety away from the continuous abuse and intimidation.

Our next move was to a much more pleasant cottage which we rented, but being short of money it was a battle trying to pay rent. By now I was at college and started working part time to help out with the rent.

As I grew up, I was not easy to live with, I found it difficult to communicate with my mother as I blamed her for all we had suffered. It seemed she was the main cause for all our problems as she had made the wrong choice in marrying and uprooting us to England. I had so much anger in me, I would often get angry and get into little rages with my mum. I would go boozing and partying with my friends and stay out all hours of the night. I also sang with bands in the clubs. My mother had no control over my life, I was what you would call a wild teenager.

At nineteen years of age I started taking marijuana. At this time, I managed to join a band where me and the main guitarist fell in love. At twenty years of age I started feeling traumatized with the life I had suffered which was an up and down spiral. By twenty-two years of age I was on hard core drugs like ecstasy and cocaine. Amazingly my boyfriend who was clean from drugs and a very light drinker was not aware of just what I had been taking. It was so easy to get my hands-on drugs. All you had to do was say that you wanted drugs and the dealer would suddenly appear, drugs were so common. I was also really clever at hiding that I had taken drugs, you learn to pretend that you are still in this world, that your feet are on the ground. I seemed so lucid that when I saw Matt, my boyfriend, he did not suspect. I was very difficult to live with, constantly angry, agitated and flying into rages. I don't know how Matt put up with me but he was always trying hard with our relationship.

Prior to starting on hard core drugs, there were numerous reasons which led me to the stage of dark despair. One of the incidents during a chapter in my life 'which tripped me over the line' was when I was working in London as a hostess. One day just before midnight when I had nearly reached home by foot, I was dragged into a passing car. As I was pulled into the car, I dropped my bag. I was so enraged that I started kicking and punching wildly. I am a strong girl and amongst all the extra skills I had learnt, one of them was boxing. The door was centrally locked when I was kicking out, I must have broken the gear box and other electronics in the car as I managed to prize the car door open. I jumped out of the running car and was so worried about my valuable bag and its contents that I first ran and picked up my bag. During my jump, I scraped my face and injured my arm and side, but I did not even notice the pain, I was numb. I than went into the nearby pub covered with blood, I must have looked a sight. But without thinking I spoke asking the men if one of them would escort me home, I would not let them call an ambulance or the police. One of the men did accompany me to my door.

Often, my way of coping with bad situations is to sleep and that's what I did, I went straight to bed without changing and went into a deep sleep. My mother was asleep and did not see the state

I was in until the morning, she was shocked. I started to get panic attacks. Also, at that time my boyfriend announced that his ex-girlfriend was pregnant. I was also in the early stages of pregnancy but suffered a miscarriage. The miscarriage caused reactive problems; the scan did not show retained products but I was haemorrhaging. I had an operation to clear out the womb. I was extremely ill and was in hospital for one month, my weight reduced to six stone. It was not an easy time, so at the age of twenty-two darkness engulfed me. Although I still tried to get on with daily life, I was a wreck, I was unbearable to those who loved me, they did not know what to do.

One day, a few years on, I decided to commit suicide. After all life just wasn't worth living, the anger in me was hard to live with. Anger and rage if not managed adequately can destroy a person. Alcohol and drugs were not having an effect on calming my emotions anymore or taking me to a place where I could shut off the real world, the fantasy world no longer existed.

There was a question of my mental health when I was six years old, I had an imaginary friend, I went for child counselling but it was decided that I just had an active imagination. No longer was my imagination the culprit. The main problem was the unbearable pain of growing up both too soon and abruptly, breaking down a soul slowly.

Life had broken me although I carried on with my daily routine and played the roles expected in normal society. What I hid well was that it was all a drudge and that everyday appeared grey. After swallowing all the tablets of codydramol and paracetamol I could get my hands on, I made a last call to a friend. He was aware of the massive argument I had had with my boyfriend and of wanting to break up with the band. He had been trying to contact me several times. After all I was not going to die quietly, I wanted someone to know! Lucky for me he realized what I had done through my slurry voice. He came over immediately and made me vomit out the medication.

After that incident I went out boozing with my friends. When I returned home in the morning, my mother realised something was wrong with me. She called an ambulance just as I fell unconscious on to the floor and stopped breathing.

People talk of an outer-body experience but all I remember in the time before I woke up is seeing darkness and the feeling of coldness all around me. I also experienced a wonderful peace and serenity that I had not felt for a long time. But instead of enjoying the peaceful feeling, I was worried about not having anything to do. The events of going to hospital or being in hospital are still not clear to me.

After discharge, I saw the GP and had cognitive counselling for six months. The counsellor was happy discharging me but I was still unsure of myself. Following the discharge, I have not wanted to take alcohol or any substances, in fact the taste of alcohol nauseates me. Amazingly my life has changed, my attitude has changed, I see life in a positive way. I have a lovely job I enjoy; I am still with the band and we are on our way to making albums. My boyfriend and I are planning a life together, he has a beautiful four-year old daughter who brings such joy to our lives. I still occasionally have little panic attacks which I am now able to control much more effectively. I have laid to rest my past and no longer feel angry or enraged about what has been. I live in the present and look forward to the future!

__Realization__

Anonymous

Inspiration was just a stigma for some people. If you help some people, joy would come automatically. But Clark didn't think that way. He thought that inspiring someone was a basic human deed – a responsibility of mankind. That it was not a favour, or something to make you feel good about yourself, it was much more than that.... Clark was reaching his fifth grade. He was the kind of person who could feel everything before any reason came his way. He saw people as they were. He didn't attach their personalities with their reasoning. Clark saw potential in everybody. And whenever he spoke the truth, people didn't like it. They had often conveyed, through their gestures, that they just saw him as rude rather than trying to convey the truth for their benefit. They excused his behaviour as lacking experience, "just a kid", they would say.

Clark was a tall boy. He was slender, when he talked, it matched the conscious politeness of his personality and good looks, added by the floating gestures of his hands. Though people saw him far from a being a bright personality, he still had an ability, although unintentionally, to wound with them with his words. His honesty and truth were like an attack. His words would always be elegant; his manners would always be sharp. And his tone, it would be agile like a kitten. He couldn't understand why people felt bad, why people were so emotional, by acknowledging that truth could benefit and put right their faults. Clark would never mask things, he just said what needed to be said. Covering up his emotions to feel good was not his thing - It was like a bad habit that felt good at first, but didn't have triumphant endeavour in the end. This he always tried to convey to his father. But his father, Jack Smith, didn't understand his boy's behaviour. He wanted him to make people happy by talking sweet instead of the hurtful truth; he wanted him to be like other kids instead of acting too mature. For Jack, it was like an urgent necessity and the final ultimatum. He needed that from Clark.

He lived in a small house, but his dreams were big. Their house was not that welcoming from the façade. The hallway wasn't wide, but everything had its sophistication. There were some childhood photographs of Jack's family in the living hall. The floor had wooden planks. Over it, the red carpet. And on the carpet, a glass table surrounded by individual sofas. The walls around the living room had the blend of a creamy colour. The small fireplace behind one of the sofas matched it. There was also a small banister, above the fireplace, that twirled. The carpenter had done his job. Though the house was small it felt soothing. It portrayed the charm that Clark had or he thought he had. But other people weren't.

Every weekend, Clark would sit on the sofa towards his right as he walked through the door. He would cross his legs, read his favourite book, and if the drops of tea fell on the glass table, he would clean the table immediately. Clark liked everything nice and clean. His father Jack couldn't understand why Clark was so neat and tidy. He would have preferred Clark to be like any normal care free boy, creating havoc and filling the house with his rowdy and mischievous laughter. Instead of driving his parents mad with school complaints, his teachers' report showed him as being the best-behaved and studious child in his school.

Every weekend, Clark and Jack would drink tea together. Jack would watch his son's face, looking tensed and worried, his forehead creasing. Clark, with his cup of tea in hand, would say in a casual tone to his dad: "What's up?"

"Nothing," his dad would reply. When Jack saw his best-behaved son clearing the mark of tea, an almost circle on the glass table, it never failed to amaze him. He would say, "I sometimes wonder if you shine the glass so well, in order to get bright ideas."

"Yes, but the teachers are not impressed with me. Even if I am top of class, the teachers prefer the other students," said Clark.

"Humans beings are very complicated. At the same time, we are an amazing species.

Your teachers say to me that you are very blunt with your answers." Jack said calmly. "But what's wrong with truth?" replied Clark

"Clark, there is nothing wrong with the truth. Sometimes the world needs an illusion. People want to feel happy even if they are not happy. Sometimes, there are no straight answers. Are you getting what I'm trying to say?" explained Jack.

Clark never saw what his father meant, "I am not going to butter people up to make them feel good" he said.

As Clark started growing up, he was ignored, except when other students needed help from him with their homework. However, he really wasn't bothered. None of it affected him emotionally. He was Clark and he expressed whatever he felt was right. This was his persona. It led to some students hating him and some admiring him.

As the months rolled by, he just didn't understand when the arc of adolescence started to hit him. There was a sudden change to his repose. His father could see the change in him; that Clark cared less about others these days. News had spread that he had started to get involved in arguments. He had started to love sports, especially, football. He didn't put the clothes as frequently in the washing machine. Sometimes he slept late and skipped school. To

Jack, all this felt normal. Sometimes during the weekends, Jack would see Clark drinking his tea very fast and hurrying out. But one day, everything changed.

Clark was sitting at his sofa, he no longer cared where he sat. His father could see that his eyes and face were red as though he had screamed. Jack watched the way Clark moved and sipped his tea while eating a bunch of chocolate cookies not caring about the crumbs on the sofa. Although Jack had wanted this, it just felt abnormal.

"Dad, I'm sick of teaching my peers calculus. But that was the only way I could talk to her."

Jack smiled. He just simply said, "What are you talking about?" Clark saw the love and understanding in his eyes. He knew his son needed someone to vent his thoughts.

"There is this girl," spoke Clark, "but she is just a friend. You see, she's not… that bright."

"And?" spoke Jack.

"And… I think that she is bright, but there are not enough actions coming from her. There is so much potential. You see—"

"Is she your girlfriend?" interrupted Jack.

"No!" exclaimed Clark. His cheeks were going red. "She is my partner… in a presentation. I want her to speak eloquently because all the parents are invited to the presentation."

"But you didn't tell me this," said Jack.

"Hmm… I'm telling you now."

Whenever he spoke with the girl, he would converse with her frankly – with truth and honesty. This had happened at first, but as the months rolled by, everything was changing. The girl didn't see him that often. It had resulted in producing more anxiety inside him. But in the classroom, she would look at him. Silence would become their communication. Her gaze would flicker on him, but in that moment, Clark would feel that her eyes were looking into his soul. He would feel insecure when the girl spoke to different people. And this had never happened to him before. He had never that experienced that feeling of jealousy before. The girl had maintained her distance from him, but she gave her cues. She was always smiling when she looked into his eyes, but now she spoke less. Even when Clark taught his peers calculus at their home, he could see the girl had started attending less classes, day by day. And the time had come when she had stopped attending his calculus classes. This made him sad. But luckily, his teachers had arranged a seminar where groups of students would do a presentation about animal rights. The girl was in his group. Clark had become nervous. And with that nervousness, he just didn't feel like doing the project. The presentation was mostly covered with words and facts. It was done by Clark himself at first. Other group members had contributed too. But the girl didn't contribute much. His group members told him the girl was contributing her talent in the form of creativity, that's why she wasn't coming to the calculus class but Clark, he didn't buy that! On the other hand, he didn't have any guts to say that in front of her. Whenever he conjured up the strength to tell her what he thought, seeing her smile at him would put a halt to him saying anything to her. Her smile was the prettiest thing he had ever seen, melting his very core, it would make him he feel awkward. This behaviour and his feelings continued till the presentation came to its finale. His group members had sent Clark the presentation file. With it, his facts and ideas changing with the amalgamation of pictures of extinct animals. Firstly, Clark didn't know what to speak about in regards to the topic because he had not put into practice what he was supposed to. Secondly, his perception was changed regarding the girl. He could see her creativity, the eloquent grace with which she had decorated the presentation for certain facts to not look boring. And when the day had arrived for the seminar, there were not only teachers and parents that were present in the auditorium room, but also some news reporters too. Every teacher had confidence that even if none of the students performed well, Clark would take over and excel. The teachers saw Clark as the backbone of everything. But this time they were wrong as he really didn't know what to do.

Every presentation had an awestruck factor with it. And when the time for his presentation came, he was just nervous. He was not the first one to speak which everyone had expected; He was the second last. Last was the girl. When Clark spoke, he didn't know what he was saying. His voice carried hesitation. He was quick to end his spot of opportunity and as the girl was last, she saw Clark's nervousness. For months, she was feeling the same kinds of feelings that Clark had toward her. Life was giving them something different to experience. And the girl was mortified with it. When her turn came to speak, Clark's eyes were wide because he saw her frozen at her spot. No words came in her mind or from her mouth. She was blankly at the audience. Some whispers too had started that revolved around the audience. Laughter came involuntarily. But at this time, Clark had conjured up the courage. He just barged onto the stage. His eyes met the girl's and he just spoke, looking at everybody.

"You see that baboon in the presentation?" he was looking at the audience with enthusiasm, "that baboon's picture has been taken from a national park. There is a curious story behind that baboon. And before I tell the story, I just wanted to tell everybody that this girl, who is standing beside me, was the one who went to that national park to take that baboon's picture. In this whole presentation that you are seeing, every animal is at the verge of extinction. These animals need our help. Every picture in the presentation is the work of this girl's creativity that you see. She might hesitate now standing in front of you all, but it is okay to be nervous," Than Clark looked at her saying, "oh, it is okay to nervous. I now understand that now everybody's truth is different," he felt deviated. Realizing it, he came back to the topic, "These animals in the present can't speak like us, but their truth is also different. We are conscious beings. We can help them. These pictures, that are taken by this girl standing beside me, tell a lot. They convey the emotion behind every animal. We all might make this presentation right now for the sake of this school, but our actions are most important to help them. This girl, who is my great friend, had gone to the National Park. She had also written a letter to them, to treat the animals, they have, properly. With her compassion... and with her great work, I want to end this presentation."

Clark stood beside her. He started applauding her, followed by everyone's claps. His father, Jack, was watching him. He finally saw a different touch of humanity, which was emotions, inside his son that he always had tried to found. For him, this realization was

an inspirational moment.

The Cycle of Life and Death.

by Sharon Bhal

It was the most traumatic period of my life when I saw my husband, Kam, suffer a stroke right in front of my eyes. The left side of his face just started drooping. Me and my elder son just looked on in horror. The change in him occurred 4 hours following an angiogram. However, when I called the nurse, she did not appear to be bothered by it but did call the cardiologist. Prior to his stroke following surgery my husband had complained of a severe headache and was given pain relief which did not make much difference to his headache. Following his surgery, he ate a sandwich and a banana. I still remember his words that the banana tasted so very delicious. Maybe that was the last thing he was ever going to eat. The last words he spoke was telling my son to take care of the family. When the doctors performed an MRI, they informed us that that my husband had suffered a stroke. The plaque in the arteries had caused a blockage. All through my husband's sickness, this was one of the scariest moments of our lives. The rest of the family came to visit in the evening. My husband had a few tubes hooked up, so he couldn't talk. But it was amazing that through this nightmare he was still able to joke and make light of his situation in order to make it easier for us. Non verbally by using his body language he told us to go home.

On the 3rd day following his stroke we got a call saying that when they had removed his breathing tube, he had suffered another major stroke and was now in a coma. The doctors performed more tests and told us that he had a brain stem stroke and that he will never be able to talk, eat, or walk again. He was in a coma for 4 days; in spite of medical reasoning he did wake up and managed to communicate non verbally especially by blinking. One blink was for yes and two blinks was for no. The doctors took us for a family meeting and said that they wanted to take my husband off the life support as there would not be any further progress. I was shocked and started biding for time. I said to the doctors before Kam makes that decision, he would like to meet his best friend and brother who lived abroad. Originally my husband had responded with a yes to being taken off the life machine. But I was adamant on changing his decision. I spoke to him of all the positivity in our life and all the positivity around. In spite of Kam lying there with a life support machine I still saw him as the man I had married and who had put so much work in our lives. He was the father of our children. I felt that no matter when, where and how it is not in our hands to take a life, that it was only God's decision to take or give life.

When his brother and friend came from abroad, we all managed to convince my husband to change his mind and reverse his decision. Even though it felt like a victory, we were happy yet sad at the same time. My husband was suffering and we were suffering with him, I also felt a sense of guilt. My husband was moved to a hospital nearer home and he lived for a further six months.

I remember the excitement when my son and his wife announced that she was expecting her first baby. My husband also expressed great excitement. There was sheer joy on his face when they found out the sex of the baby, and then we saw the deflation on his face with sadness as he expressed that he would not see or hold his grandson. But I also knew that moments like this could not be replaced, just seeing that joy on his face was worth it. It made me see he was still living.

I was always there by Kam's bedside talking to him, caring for him, and my family were there often too. I think he felt loved and supported. After a life time of being with someone, you understand their needs and you can often anticipate their thoughts. My husband and I understood each other. Even though he could not talk we communicated a great deal, probably even more than we did during our busy periods in our life when he was healthy.

On 8th January Kam passed away. On hearing the news, although expecting that the inevitable would one day happen, it was as if my world had fallen apart. I must have screamed so loudly that my son who was in the elevator heard me. The loss of their father and the events leading to the loss led my children to question God and to lose faith, but my faith remained strong. During the cremation I was about to cry when I felt a spiritual calmness around me.

Bereavement following the death of my husband bought sadness and depression. Days felt dark and every day was a trudge. I could not enjoy the little things in life. I did not know how I would get through life. After 3 months our first grandson was born, which was a bitter sweet moment. As I held my grandson in my arms, looking at his beautiful face, I felt my world light up again and felt my depression lift.

- "The Miracle of life!".

After Retirement
By Judy Saunders

Having worked for more than 45 years for the same company and then facing the prospect of retirement, I asked myself "what can I do now"? I have always been a doer and just loved to help others, I was in a job where my help was constantly sought.

Once I completed some of the outstanding jobs needing to be done for quite some time at home, I decided I should apply to volunteer for various organisations.

I had cared for my elderly mother before retirement, albeit latterly she was in a Nursing Home, but I used to go in and visit and help regularly with activities. I found my time there helping other carers very rewarding, from helping the mobile hairdresser to joining in with bingo and singing with the residents. Some residents would just prefer to stay in their rooms, but once all together they enjoyed their time.

I realised then that many volunteers came to the Nursing Home giving up their time, even while still working, and that extra help was needed just to ease the pressure on staff and also to families who often struggled to visit their elderly relative.

Voluntary work was where I thought I should concentrate utilising my free time. Our local Alzheimer's Dementia Support (ADS) group were looking for help to support people and contacted the Manager to arrange a meeting and discuss where I could best fit in. One option was to become a befriender to take a dementia sufferer out for a coffee or to a meeting group who otherwise could not go out and allowing the family carer time for themselves for a few hours. I needed to attend two training courses, one on the rules of befriending and one on safeguarding.

My first lady allocated to me had been a ballroom dancer in her younger days. The ADS group holds a meeting regularly called Moves and Grooves for anyone wanting to go dancing.

I picked up my lady, who was extremely nervous as she didn't know me at all and really only wanted to stay with her family at home. With encouragement and reassurance, we headed to the venue and waited for the volunteer professional dancer to put the music on and encourage people onto the floor. My lady had her dancing shoes with her and once she heard the music was up and dancing rumba's, samba's, waltz loving every minute. It was such a pleasure to see her enjoying herself and talking about her time back home with her dancing partners and reminiscing. She could remember and perform every step.

It was very hard to accept that once we left the venue, my lady could not remember being there or where we were going next, her anxieties had returned. But for that hour in time she was happy and relaxed and enjoying the very thing she loved.

Her family were so grateful to have an afternoon to themselves, to do what they wanted without the worry of their mother being left on her own at home.

My second dementia patient was a gentleman in his 80's who liked to go for walks. He had completely lost the ability to communicate and his poor wife naturally needed a well-earned rest to go shopping and leave the house without worrying about her husband.

We went out to a local beauty spot to walk amongst the lovely grounds. He tells me what he remembered living at home in Barbados with his mother and father and sisters. He could recall how they used to pick fruit and the family made cakes. Sadly, that's all I could find out about him in the two hours together. He couldn't tell me what he had done for a living for the majority of his working life, what his wife's name was or his children's names. But he enjoyed every minute of being out and talking about his life back home as a child. I also took him to the Carers Cafe to a singing group for Dementia sufferers. It was soon evident that all the attendees without exception, all the people there could remember every word of every song without the music sheet.

I have found this experience very rewarding and feel I have gained a good insight into the extremely upsetting world of dementia sufferers who are locked into a time where they can remember experiences from their youth but little else.

Alongside joining ADS group, I have spent two years volunteering at the Brett Foundation, a charity which provides breakfast and meals to the local vulnerable people in the community, from the homeless to people with mental health issues. The facilities are very limited but are able to provide a basic breakfast and a hot drink and a place to meet for two hours each morning. Again, very rewarding to know you can make a difference for a short time each day where people relied upon the sanctuary of a warm place to sit and chat.

I also started cooking a hot meal once or twice a month to provide an evening meal for the users. Not being a chef, I found this quite testing. Having to increase cooking for two to maybe 25 people who could drop in. Without exception every person expressed their appreciation for the warm food and was so grateful, especially in the winter months, either not having a home to cook in or to afford the supplies they needed.

At Christmas time the Foundation also organised a Shoe Box Appeal for local residents to donate a box of various items to be wrapped in Christmas paper which were then sent out to Sierra Leone to be distributed to the young children living in isolated communities. Families and schools were very generous bringing into the centre their boxes, providing small items of clothes, pens, pencils, sweets. We were able to see a video of the delivery and the children queuing to receive their box of goodies. It felt heart-warming knowing that so many people had helped and had made a huge difference.

So now we are mostly isolating ourselves with the worldwide spread of the Coronavirus which has swept into our lives, closing down shops, transport, schools and at this moment mostly all on lockdown. I cannot volunteer now with the organisations I have been associated with and to help the most vulnerable, as I am in that most vulnerable age bracket. I cannot now go out and help anyone. This is very hard for me and everyone to accept and come to terms with.

If we all follow the Government rules imposed and stay at home and don't mix with our family or friends, then just hopefully we will get through this sooner rather than later. This is changing all our lives and is an unprecedented situation. I hope you all stay safe and life will be back to normal in the coming months.

Spiritual Stirring

BY Gille Sidhu

No matter where you go is a clear path set, a destiny which takes you where you need to be!

Some people simply want to concentrate on their physical life, having fun, their career etc. and want to let sleeping dogs lie when it comes to the spiritual side of life. Other people have the ability to use their spirituality to link with a world that others are not able to. However, there are many phenomena shared by people of all cultures worldwide. For some it is a minor event such as something falling in the kitchen which cannot be explained or just an experience, a very pleasant or unpleasant feeling which is put down to intuition or the tricks our mind plays on us. How many people have sensed the presence of our loved ones, have the light suddenly turned off in the room, seen little sparkly lights! Some of us are too frightened to talk, in case others think we are crazy.

There is a belief that science has an explanation for everything, but does it really?

I still remember when I was a student nurse, a lovely man was brought in from the streets to our ward, when… I met him, he was in a hospital gown and looked presentable. As he was a patient, I became aware that he was homeless. When I chatted to him, he said he was a traveler, and could tell any time of the day without looking at a watch. Of course, I was curious and questioned him about the time, he confirmed the correct time to the second. You may wonder if there was a clock in the room, no there was no clock in his line of vision! He went on to tell me what was going on in my life at the time and what my parents were doing which was concerning me. I found everything he told me to be true. So strange, that a man I had never met before and was never to meet again could be so accurate about what was going on in my life and my thoughts. I was quite amazed.

As I was bringing up young children, I had decided to work nights during the first few years of working in the hospice. The only staff on night duty were either two or three nurses, sometimes people stayed overnight with their loved one, especially during the latent terminal stages. All the rooms in the hospice were individual single rooms. The atmosphere in the day was peaceful but filled with activity, however at night, after the initial activity when the lights in the corridor were dimmed, there was a cutting silence which was at times interrupted by sounds such as the phone or buzzers from the room of patients. I felt a warm comfort in having a colleague working with me, but when the colleague was at her break and the patients were sleeping the silence could be intense.

Most supernatural experiences happened after dusk when the atmosphere was most quiet and dreams could be felt in the air. As I did my rounds down the long corridor in order to make sure the patients were comfortable, I would feel goosebumps and at times the hair standing on end on my arms and a chill in the air. Other times there would just be a warm peaceful feeling around me and as if a pleasant whispered secret was in the air.

One day a couple of nurses appearing very excited got my attention. They told me that the tea-towels in the kitchen had come flying off from the rail on the wall. I wondered if they could have just dropped from the rails, but they insisted that the tea towels actually flew across the room a fair way before landing on the floor. The incident would give us food for thought. Did both nurses have an active imagination or was this an unseen energy?

A woman, terminally ill and taking her last breath, mentioned that she saw a man with a horse and carriage come to pick her up. Her close relatives were by the bedside at the time when I entered the room. They seemed to believe what she was saying. The strange thing was that when I was a child, one of the stories my mother told me and my siblings, was about my grandmother when she stopped breathing one day, it happened when my mother was still very young. Thinking their mother had died both my mum and her siblings were crying over their mother's body when a few minutes later she woke up. On waking up my grandmother told her story and said that a man with a horse and carriage had come to pick her up, but when she was about to get into the carriage the man said 'you had better go back', your children are still young and need you. He told her that it was not her time to die, after which she found herself back in her body waking up to the faces of her children crying over her.

The nurses 'rest room' where we took our breaks, appeared to take on a different atmosphere at night. We found that if we dozed off in the room during our break, me and my colleagues would experience weird dreams and even nightmares. The strange thing was that both me and a couple of colleagues could hear our names being called at the end of our breaks should we doze off.

One night after returning from my break, I did my rounds. Satisfied that all the patients were comfortable and sleeping, I sat down behind the nursing station. That night, my eyes felt particularly heavy causing my eyelids to droop. No sooner had my eyes closed when I heard a gentle yet authoritative voice calling out my name. Startled I looked up and saw a figure with a nuns clothing standing across from me-I could barely make out her face; within seconds she glided down the corridor. Although frightened I stood up following her but she simply faded and vanished into thin air. I would have put it down to my imagination or a hallucination had not the patients mentioned seeing a nun standing at the foot of their beds.

How many people do you know who show you the wonders of life? It doesn't matter if they are religious or simply a passerby whose identity you do not know. The light shines through them giving you hope and making you feel that much stronger. For me, one of those was a lovely priestess who was admitted to the hospice in the latent stages. She was hunched over, but I have never seen such an independent soul. Although she experienced a great deal of pain she would insist on washing and dressing herself and walking with a stick. Her pain tolerance was very high. One day she even went out to baptize a child-I remember her leaving the ward full of purpose and returning, clambering into her bed exhausted but still with a vibrancy that said 'I am OK'! However, it did take its toll on her and very soon in the following days she laid down to take her last breaths. In the night before reaching the end of her life she asked a nurse to read passages to her from the bible. As the nurse was reading, she experienced a strong gush of breeze in the room even though the windows were closed. The nurse was someone who would not normally talk about the supernatural, and if any of our colleagues would share a story, he did not want to hear and would walk away. In the early hours of the morning the priestess asked me for more pain relief-when… I went to draw up her pain relief, she had taken her last breath. She looked so peaceful although she had died alone. There is a theory that sometimes we wait for a loved one to come to us but other times we wait for people to leave before taking our last breaths. In my experience in the hospice, I feel that nothing is a coincidence. When we die the person or people present during our last moments on earth were meant to be there. In the case of the priestess, I questioned the fact that she had indeed died alone. I did not feel she was alone when I saw her peaceful serene face. I was aware of a vibrant energy in the room which suggested to me a presence I was unable to see.

Sometimes we learn so much without a word being said and others times others can lecture you and you learn not a thing. This alone in itself is a phenomenon!

Ten years of working in a hospice can change a person. Maybe it was working in an environment where the unknown gives off an energy, almost like an invisible gentle electric current. Most people accepted this current as a normal, unseen phenomena, they may comment on feeling a chill or feeling weird, but otherwise there never was a discussion. I don't know when it all started, was it working in the hospice, or did I always possess a sensitivity to my environment and the sensitivity just heightened over time. I found it easier to pick up emotions and the pain of others. There were times when I would be extremely sensitive to the pain of others and did not know how to protect myself from my environment, leaving myself exhausted. I used to go into the hospice happy and by the end of the shift on days I would leave extremely sad and drained of emotion. There were times when I was resilient to emotional pain, almost as a protection and a means to survive. This continued until I changed jobs.

After changing jobs, I continued to feel the effects of emotions from the patients. I was told by a psychic that I had a gift of being able to help heal and that I could be a healer if I put my mind to it. I know that sometimes sitting next to a friend who had not yet conveyed their feelings to me I would feel their pain, emotional or physical. I could feel myself being drawn to people's pain. If someone had a headache, I would perform a couple of minutes shiatsu on their neck and head and would be informed that they felt better. I am aware that working in the hospice my psychic abilities were heightened, ever since then I have used these in positively supporting others.

I feel this psychic ability more acutely when I am peaceful and tuned in to the tranquility of nature. During my ventures, after working in the hospice, I was able to tune in to the healing energy around me. Although I had learned some shiatsu during my time in the hospice and used my skills to help various physical ailments, I never thought of myself as a healer. I don't think I chose to be a healer; nature chose me to heal.

Every time I sit high on a mountain, I feel the wonderful energy in the air. I do find that the positive energy is really vibrant on the mountains and if we tune in to the energy we can do so much. Having travelled to villages in Indonesia as a health worker, I came across a beautiful village in Indonesia called Taniwoda. Our hostess in the village complained she had fallen and broken a bone in her finger a few weeks ago and the pain was still quite intense. I took her finger in my hand and intuitively applied some gentle pressure and stretches on her finger. After a couple of minutes of applying pressure she said her finger felt much better. On a further trip to the village she said that the pain had never returned and she felt her finger had healed. She then went on to recommend me to other people in the village and I became known as a healer in the Taniwoda and surrounding villages.

Of course, we need to have that inner conviction that life is amazing and we love and want to help others. I have always been drawn towards wanting to help people but has healing others always been part of me, or is it an energy that is present for periods of times? I once read that we all have the ability to heal ourselves. If we have the right empathy, can we all be healers? Or is it something beyond our comprehension, that unseen spiritualness which comes across as an energy which surrounds us and sometimes sends sensations causing our skin to tingle.

That continuous interest in the unknown has led me to experience new endeavors. Once I decided to try Shamanism. I searched and found a venue in Scotland, out high in the mountains. It was in the middle of winter. As I sat on the plane and closed my eyes, I saw two very deep sharp eyes staring at me. It was a tall handsome man with dark eyes, prominent features and wearing a black hat. During the Shamanism weekend I felt a very strong energy. When we were healing, everyone commented that they could feel the healing energy from me and felt healed from the pain they were suffering. While on the mountains I felt connected to the spiritual world. After coming back from Scotland, I felt that I was very strong. I felt a kind of power which I had not felt before. People around me were very attentive. I had a sensation of feeling powerful, I had brought that feeling with me from the weekend in Scotland. Both at work and at home I was being listened to but I did not feel right about it. There was something sinister in this new found power. Somehow, I had a strong prompting feeling that I had a been given a choice between two paths; One path would lead me towards material gain and power, the other path would lead me to spiritual peace and contentment.

In my life I have enjoyed responsibility and caring for others and have never felt the need of power or control. I have always had my feet firmly on the ground and I have always followed my instinct and intuition which can grow with experience. I consciously made the choice of following the second path of tuning myself to nature rather than focusing on wealth and power.

We all make our choices by choosing what we want to believe, but sometimes we come face to face with the unknown and see beyond the presented scientific facts....

I feel the vibration of the energy around me, the healing energy connecting us to each other and the unknown.

Nostalgia
by Gille Sidhu

You often don't realize just how wonderful and valuable it is when you are in the middle of that once-in-a- lifetime experience. You go through the days and weeks doing what needs to be done, taking things for granted and forget to see the real beauty around you. Today I sat and looked through the volunteers' magazine, saw the faces that had been a part of my life for almost two years. There were volunteers that came and went, and there were volunteers that stayed the duration of my time in Indonesia. I did not realize the buzz of having likeminded friends all around Indonesia who wanted to do good for the country and who wanted to do good generally in life. Such is the energy that is so vibrant. There are times that can be despairing but the positive attitude kept everyone going, the ongoing support was amazing! We have expectations of people close to us, being there, and helping us through our troubled times. But in actual fact, every kindness shown to us and us showing kindness to others has a great positive impact on the world. Everything and everyone are definitely connected. The connection was obvious when I felt the vibrancy of the adventure experienced over a decade ago. I wondered about the growth of the mangroves we planted, the cleaning of the sea of deadly jelly fish. So many thoughts I have so much to say!

Coming back to England, life just continued. Was it me that had chilled out or did people around me, especially at work, become more stressed? Power and struggle keeping the joy at bay! Passing comments, I made of my adventure to those who listened, but motivation laid to rest. Blending into life again as a professional, work with compassion continued. Lost amongst fulfilling the responsibilities of the present, the needs of friends left behind becoming more in the distance and less of a priority. The 'Now' is always the focus of our attention, struggling in the present to do our best. But reminiscing through the photos of the days as a volunteer, the sleeping past became a reality. Suddenly the nostalgia settled in taking me back to that time of old, just like the time traveler back in the past.

A niggly feeling and then it all began. With the world tragedy; the tsunami, making my feet itching to go, go to a land needing to be built on. To cater to basic needs, bringing them nearer to the life of those living with much more ease, raising the standard of good health.

I said farewell with a smile to those I cared about and those dependent on me. Now they will stand on their own two feet. For two years I am away, feeling a call leading the way. VSO (volunteering services abroad) paving the way.

As I walked on the land of Bali, people were so welcoming and I met my new colleagues. We had six weeks of training in the Indonesian language. Nothing is ever really learnt until utilizing the lessons and turning the lessons into experience. I struggled but just about managed to communicate in Indonesian with broken language, using an English accent and body language to explain. I am sure it must have been irritating to some. I remember in Bali, when I was learning the local language, the girls behind the shop counters would turn away from me to their colleagues and snigger. It just made me more determined to speak until I was understood.

After my training in Bali, I had a little time to kill so decided to be a lone traveler. I visited the Gili Islands and decided to go on a snorkeling tour where they took us further down towards the deeper part of the beautiful blue sea. We all jumped in. The fish were so colorful with different patterns and varied from small to moderate sizes, swimming round the coral reefs, the sea rougher than I liked. After swimming for a while, I decided to go back to the boat. I wasn't too far from the boat when I felt that I was swimming and not getting anywhere. It was a weird sensation. I felt sure I was making progress but the boat remained the same distance. A woman fairly near me called out about the danger we were in, being caught up in a current. "Swim sideways" she shouted"! A stronger swimmer, she got to the boat before me and handed me the rope. Amazingly no one else noticed that we were in …danger, if… we had drowned would we have been missed? But the laughable fact was what the headlines would have been 'Gille drowned in Gili Island'!

Landing on the soil of Flores over the waters not far from Bali, landing in a little city called Ende. A city in which I was to live, different from what I knew. Flores, a land not fully built, sometimes nature's disasters caused the hit, each time causing destruction and sorrow. Motor bikes everywhere, food markets from the farming villages were held in the morning. Shops were not up to standard of the western world, as wares were scarce. People were different, more laid back with life. Locals not speaking a word of English, what I thought common language to be, the language spoken worldwide. How sheltered had I been? So very used to the comfort of family and friends and of a busy life. Racing against time, television also to pass my time, a constantly busy mind, losing the concept of who I am. Growing up in a world of noise, it was unheard of sitting silently and simply externalizing and internalizing the environment. As dusk settled in, sitting and staring at the open sea, a person often by my side, but the silence and idleness spelled loneliness for me.

I was given a title of a Health coordinator when working with the local NGO (non-governmental organization). The NGO had projects to develop the villages, up in the mountains, in order to improve their agriculture and economics. Realizing the need of Health Education, VSO first bought in a nutritionist who moved on to different ventures as I stepped in as a health educator. Only temporary in that place, I aimed for my colleagues to learn to improve health and continue the work for those who need. New Colleagues and local people were friendly and willing to learn, but first I had to bridge the gap of the language barrier. Those who could speak English, out of embarrassment, were too self-conscious to practice and speak English for fear of making a fool of themselves, as it was a culture that sought perfection. The first challenge was for me to speak the native tongue fluently.

After the settling-in period I realized it was not at all bad. The highlight for me was riding on the back of a motor bike, up the mountain, with the cool breeze hitting my face on a hot humid day. The winding road leading to the villages surrounded with beauty, occasional huts on the road, the greenery, the deep valleys, sometimes monkeys would show themselves. The real challenge came when we were off the road on rocky, bumpy, narrow paths. If not careful, our fate would be a long drop making it the last trip. Especially the village Taniwoda, one of the villages based highest on that mountain.

The road to Taniwoda is very long and hard, but certainly not tedious and boring. Each time I have travelled, it was just that more broken and dangerous. It is not possible for a car to get through to get to the village. I shudder at the thought of what happened in an emergency. Reliant on the driver's skill, because there was an unshakeable fear that the journey could have been the last. When we reached the village, the friendly souls invited us in. As the night set in, the moon lit the sky and it seemed that I could touch the stars.

Maybe it was a blessing in disguise, an experience I would like to share. Once a colleague was teaching me to ride a motorbike. I have never ridden even a bike when growing up, now in my forties I was learning to ride a motorbike. The feeling which I cannot describe, was one of excitement and heart in mouth. After practising in a field, my colleague took me for a test run on the road. Apprehensive yet I was delighted. His advice to me was always to look in the direction I was travelling in, but I took his advice further still. As I was driving down a curvy road, I carried on straight towards the pavement as my eyes settled on a walking man. As if in a trance, my bike, obliging my gaze, carried on straight with my hands stiff on the handlebars. Horrified, my colleague on the back seat, shouted for me to stop, but it did not register in the mind of mine. I went straight towards the man missing him by inches as he crouched on the floor with the back of his hand shielding his face, his eyes glazed with fear, the fence touching his back, he was stuck with nowhere to move. I stopped inches from him, 'poor man' shaking with fright, he had nothing to say! Feeling shocked I don't remember an apology coming from my mouth. My colleague never again trusted me to lead the bike. It was definitely a blessing in disguise, as I would have taken the risk of riding the motorbike on unavoidable dangerous paths, without knowing the skills the locals used.

I saw those people aiming to thrive, struggling to grow amongst the world, but first they had to fulfill their basic needs before their wants.

Each person possesses individual dreams of wanting more. But even dreams and motivation cannot always overcome the barriers of being born in poverty, without outside help of those who have!

Worldly comforts went down the hatch, when you stayed in the villages, three days at a time. They were generous cooking food. Luckily, I was a vegetarian and got away from eating dog, a food cooked on special occasions. Syrupy tea and homemade spirit also offered in hospitality as a routine to the guest. Difficult to say no as you did not want to offend. Water was not available in some of the villages. The locals, often children, had to walk a minimum mile or two to bring the water from the spring. Weather could range from extreme stormy rain to unbearable heat, crops often felt the pinch.

Understanding that each and every one has similar needs and have their own personalities of what they want, especially the youth who wanted more. We would sit around the fire discussing each and everything. The mountains cool at night and the feeling of warmth glowed within. Such lovely people, their generosity and the love they gave. Have you ever danced on a mountain?

They made the effort to make us feel welcome, no matter how much they possessed, they always gave. The experience would humble those whom thought themselves superior.

I wondered why they lived in places where resources were scarce. One day I was taken to an old man who told me a story of the darkest days. His face rugged through wearing age, in actual fact he was near the mark of hundred but still agile. He spoke in his local dialect Lio, translated by a friend. He explained why people had built their homes so far into the mountain. First came the Portuguese, making slaves of the locals, people escaped into mountains, then came the Christians, converting the locals to be Christians. Anyway, the old man told his story of the barbaric treatment by the Japanese, the atrocities suffered by the indigenous people when they took over the city Maumere. The torture, massacre and rape, enslaving people such an unbearable thought. In order to escape they fled from the city deep into the mountains and learned to eat anything they could get their hands on.

Although it all happened many moons ago, it's sad to think of all the locals had suffered, many countries suffered ill fates where they were victims by those so unfeeling. Power so misused during war where soldiers had become brainwashed and treated humans like parasites.

High in the mountains, women lacked antenatal care, not travelling to hospitals due to a fear of death. One community midwife was allocated to many villages, she was not seen by most who needed. Local women were often the attendants to birth. Mortality and morbidity high, lack of care, illness and disease, causing needless pain. Disability of children and mental health a hidden thing. We attempted to educate and make a plan in order to lessen the desperation.

Through innovative ways, developing the work of Kaders (local supporters of the mother and child clinics called a posyandu), we monitored the growth and nutrition of the child. The colleagues all worked hard combining programs of health, agriculture and economics hand in hand. Workshops and meetings on various topics were held, encouraging women to leave their household duties and attend. With the local government's help, skin problems being one of the major problems, children in the villages were treated.

The biggest conference of 5 days was held in the village involving professionals from far and wide. Sanitation had increased by folds in the villages. Measures by the external evaluators shown, it reached higher than the expected mark. My colleagues each now skilled in health and environment, were dedicated to continue till the end, implementing projects in new rural villages. My sisters fund raised, sons and close friends supported the work in many ways. Successful development is never done by one person in a land, it takes a great deal of people behind the scenes and a great deal of education in order to use those natural resources each person and the land possess. Effective planning and hard work as a team is a must!

Going over the mountain on a bimo mini bus to the resort of nature in Maurere, I came to hear, of the miracle of a grandchild to be born. The word came from the air and spirit of the mountain into my mind. I shared the thought to a friend, amazingly soon a call came from my son, announcing that a future birth was inevitable.

My work accomplished in Ende, I was sad to leave such a lovely land, but made my way home as I would not miss the birth of my grandchild. Another story to be told.

Why Clothing Became My Armour In Which I Battled The World

By Hayley

I love the feeling putting on a nice dress gives me. It makes me feel special and it fills me with confidence. Ultimately clothing and the feeling it gave me, helped me survive in that funny thing we call life. Not in the way you'd imagine.

My Story

Once upon a time life wasn't so kind and the people in it weren't either.

I am a survivor of domestic abuse. I am a proud of who I am today. I do not describe myself as a victim, survivor suits me best.

Survivors are brave people. I can't commend them enough. It takes every bit of strength in your body to not only survive during your experience but the aftermath too. It takes an incredible amount of courage to leave, something I could not have done alone.

Surviving can be very misunderstood. The abuse you have experienced doesn't just stop when you leave. In fact, a survivor is more at risk when an abuser loses control of their victim. Irrational behaviour can escalate, it did in my case. There is also the battle in your mind that you deserved to be treated a certain way. You look to rationalise, and you simply can't. Your mind is filled with negative thoughts about who you are and what you have been through.

Never and I mean never is the abuse you have experienced ever your fault. This is something I had to remind myself of daily.

The negative thoughts were there whilst in the relationship, so it wasn't something new. The survival battle isn't for the faint-hearted. I believe this is a contributing factor as to why people return.

People talk about big life events, sadly this is one of mine. The abuse I suffered was both physical and emotional.

An abuser will use many manipulative tactics to bully you and remain in control. Physical violence, isolation, keeping you away from your friends and family. They may also use your children as a form of control. Threaten to report you to professional bodies or take your children away and not return them, they may play down their violence or bullying and even manipulate children. I know the signs oh so well.

There is no 'on' switch as to when it happens. I can only describe it as like a whirlpool that slowly draws you in. Little by little you get pulled ever so slowly, unnoticeable until you arrive at what I can only describe as hell. Treading on eggshells becomes the norm. It all becomes normalised existence.

Your day to day living is about nothing else other than surviving. Not aggravating your abuser. You must think about everything you say, as you fear it could be wrong. Eventually there is nothing left of you. You live in fear. Fear of out bursts. You live your life on someone else's terms and conditions. The goal posts are constantly moved and what might be acceptable one day, isn't another. It confuses you.

Mentally it breaks you to stay but it also breaks you to leave. After all isn't this love? You are trauma bonded to someone you think will change. It or the abuse never does. It is a never-ending cycle unless you break it.

When you leave, the world and his wife have an opinion.

'You don't look like someone that has been abused.'

'It couldn't have been that bad or you would have left.'

'It must be lies'

'What did you do to cause this?'

I have heard it all

Smear campaigns are a reality. If anyone has been on the end of one its cruel. People dislike you, think you are to blame. I have been laughed at. I have been accused of being a liar. Victim blaming exists in this world, sadly.

Smear campaigns exist as when someone cannot control you anymore, they will control how others see you. Powerful isn't it!

I count myself lucky in my case there was a conviction. When I say that out loud it sounds rather bizarre, for some sadly that doesn't happen. Can you imagine going through this horrendous experience and not ever seeing justice? It can be very much a reality.

Survivors are strong people. I don't mean in the physical sense I mean mentally. Taking control back of your life after going through domestic abuse takes an amazing amount of courage. Survivor's lived horrendous conditions all whilst painting on that smile. Imagine living that every day.

Trying to hold your head high from you have been through this isn't easy. You grieve for a life, which you didn't realise was a lie. Remember this daily existence is 'normal.' Learning to think for yourself, it is like learning to walk again. You do lose things, material things, friends (remember the smear campaign) but you gain so much. You gain FREEDOM.

When I initially left my confidence was low, people were laughing at me, I was the lady that people had formed an opinion on. When I spoke, I used to look at the floor. I never felt the need to justify why I left or to put my story across. Those that know, know the reality. For those that don't, I simply hope they never go through the experience I went through or find themselves in a situation like I found myself in.

As the years go by, I can now relate to others like me. There is a secret survivor appreciation code. We salute one another and realise what beautiful strong people we all are.

Help is always there

When I finally made the decision to leave, I had the amazing support of Caron and The DASH Charity. The DASH team were like having a best friend, they provided education and helped me understand what was happening to me. I believe this education helped me to make the best life choices for myself and my children, ultimately helped me to become a survivor.

What did I do?

Life carries on around you despite what I was experiencing or how you are feeling. I had to make the decision to sink or swim. I chose to swim.

I ignored people's opinions and laughter, of course at times I wanted to shout and scream from the rooftops. But what was the point?

Instead I went about my daily routine. I put my best dress on. I walked taller and smiled harder. It is the most empowering thing I could do. I smiled in the face of fear! I smiled so hard I never looked back.

I am now an ambassador to the wonderful DASH Charity; I support them in many ways including raising funds and by telling my story. My hope that if someone hears or reads my story they may not feel alone. It may give them the strength to ask for help. Domestic Abuse can be the loneliest existence there is, I hope to change that.

I now look back on my experience positively. I wouldn't be the strong woman I am today without it.

Special thanks to Caron and The DASH Charity for helping to reclaim my freedom.

Supporting a Charity

Fighting against

Abuse & Victimisation

Proceeds to go to the

DASH CHARITY

(Domestic Abuse Stops Here)

Printed in Poland
by Amazon Fulfillment
Poland Sp. z o.o., Wrocław

64125263R00094